LAND OF DEEP WATERS

Patricia M. Robertson

The house was on fire. She could smell the smoke, feel it choking her in her sleep, feel the heat. There was also the smell of blood, hot and sticky, unmistakable. She could taste it. She jumped out of bed, hurried down the stairs and out the door. Her sons were with her. Somehow she got them out safely. Then she woke.

She listened for the sound of her smoke detector–nothing. False alarm. Beside her, Dave slept peacefully, undisturbed by her dream. Quietly she slipped out of bed lest she disturb him. She walked downstairs and into the kitchen of their split-level home, seeking water. It seemed the smell of smoke was still around, scorching her parched throat. The dream had been that real. And blood, she felt the need to wash her hands to flush away the stench and gulp down water to rinse the taste from her mouth. After assuring herself that there was no fire about to burst out of their basement, she sat to finish off the glass.

What was it all about? What did it mean? She recognized the house, even though it had been years since she had been there. It was owned by the Dominican sisters in Tegucigalpa, capital of Honduras. She remembered it very well from her years spent in ministry there. She remembered the simple, two-story home with white walls, an open stair case and rocking chairs. There were rocking chairs everywhere, located on the balcony, in the living room, one in each bedroom, designed for those who would rock and reflect. The house was filled with simple designs, simple colors – white and brown, natural browns of wood, wooden crosses on the walls in each room, wooden tables and chairs in the dining room, high-back chairs. Is it any wonder it burned so thoroughly?

It had been many years since she had been there. She had lived several lives since then. What did it mean? Whose blood was it? And why were her boys with her, school aged, not in their twenties as they actually were? In her dreams they had been but six and nine. It has been a long time since they were so young. It had been a long time since she was so young, since she had been in Honduras.

Joan waited for the sound of a phone ringing to break the silence. Surely someone was hurt, she thought. That was the reason her dream was so vivid: It was a warning. But the phone didn't ring and eventually she talked herself back into bed to while away the remaining hours till dawn. Her mind returned to those years in Honduras long ago, events not forgotten. How could she forget those incidents? They remained emblazoned in her mind, reminders of the destructive nature of humanity. Had she gotten out in time? In time to save herself and the sons she eventually had? She didn't know. And what of the children that had been left behind? The children of the campesinos?

She had been a newly professed sister, anxious to begin her life as a missionary. She was able to spend a summer during her novitiate with sisters in Peru. It only served to heighten her determination to come back to the missions. And so it was arranged for her to live in community with two of their sisters serving in the diocese of Olancho, Honduras. She could hardly wait for the adventure to begin. She stepped off the plane into another world, a world full of machine guns slung onto the shoulders of police lining the airport. Welcome to Honduras, land of deep waters, she thought. What a welcoming committee, yet an appropriate welcome/warning as she learned later. But then she was greeted by Sr. Anita and Sr. Rosa and swept away to the convent in Juticalpa. She had been eager to get started, but their trip had been delayed by a meeting that was to take place there.

"It will be a good opportunity to meet some of the other sisters working in Olancho, as well as some of the brothers and priests," Anita had dutifully informed her. "And you have to meet Nick, the bishop."

It seemed she wasn't the only newcomer about to begin ministry in Olancho. Two priests who had driven down from the states were expected that night.

Joan hoisted her backpack and suitcase, all her worldly possessions, all she had to last her for however long she would be here. She had been told to pack light, and she had complied. Just the barest necessities, clothes, a few books, her Bible, her journal, her Spanish-English dictionary and toiletry items were the sum total of her riches. Everything else she would either have to do without or purchase out of her small monthly allowance. But she wasn't concerned. She had managed just fine for two months in Peru with just what she carried on her back. In contrast to that, what she had now felt like a wealth of goods. She also expected it would appear like riches to those among whom she would be serving.

The two priests arrived in time for dinner. They had driven through the night, and were still recovering from the trip and lack of sleep.

They seemed nice enough, if poorly prepared. One, Fr. Paul, fidgeted all through dinner, complaining about the butt-busting trip they had just completed, driving through Mexico. His sandy brown hair had been cut close to the skin around the ears with just a bit of length on the top which he ran his hand through periodically. He also sported what appeared to be a beard, short and close-cropped, and almost imperceptible against his fair complexion. He was tall, slender and young. She remembered how young both he and his partner appeared, even though older than her by at least two years.

His buddy, Fr. Kevin, had a darker complexion, clean shaven with longish, dark brown hair. He was shorter and stouter than Paul but every bit as young. Their Spanish was almost non-existent. She had been surprised by this. What had they been thinking?

"Once we get settled in and immersed in the language, I'm sure it will come quickly," Kevin stated. Paul merely grunted in quiet disagreement. "Besides, I've had enough of school. I'm ready to do something." Now Paul appeared to be in agreement with that.

The drive from the U.S. had been necessary, she soon found out, because of all they had brought with them. Their truck had been loaded with supplies, donations for their ministry that they just knew they would not be able to get along without, or at least so Kevin said. He already had plans for the orphanage he dreamed of building. He even had a list of donors whom he could tap for money.

"I can't wait to get started. We've got medical supplies for a clinic, a generator for those inevitable power outages, and once we get settled we plan to start an orphanage."

He was the more talkative of the two and was eager to regale them with his stories of their trip down and their plans. Paul was more taciturn, excusing himself as he stood to stretch his legs and light a pipe, emitting a distinguished air, or so it appeared he thought. The parish priest, Fr. Eduardo, had joined them for dinner. He politely rounded up his two charges and took them back to the cathedral rectory for the night.

During breakfast the sisters were joined by two more from their order and then they proceeded to the parish center for the meeting with Bishop Nick. Joan was pleased to see the two young priests again. Even if she had sworn off marriage, it was still enjoyable to spend time with someone closer to her age.

She felt so old when she crawled out of bed. Already she was experiencing stiffness related to arthritis. Her bones were showing signs of aging and the eventual need for surgery. How she wished to be young again, to move freely, be active, abuse her body without paying for it immediately. How she longed for adventure, adventures like she had had in Honduras. She longed to travel, see the world again, but would her body let her? Would she be able to tolerate sleeping on hard floors or cots in youth hostels? Would they even let her in? Her sons were grown, didn't need her any more, off on adventures of their own. It was time for her to have new adventures, but where, when and how?

She looked over at her sleeping husband. Steady, reliable, he was always there for her. She could count on him, but not for adventure, not for thrills and excitement. She would never be able to convince him to travel beyond Florida. That was his idea of adventure, driving every winter to Florida to escape the snow. If she were to go, she would have to go alone, or drag Dave behind her. It would be easier just to go by herself, but where and when and to what purpose? She wanted, needed, a plan. Her days of aimless wandering were over. She didn't want to risk not having a place to sleep each night or a source of food. She sounded just like Dave – he must have rubbed off on her somewhere along the course of their life together.

She hated her life, so predictable, so comfortable, so . . . middle class! When had she sold out? Had she sold out? When and where had she left her ideals along the way? Too many years had slipped by. She had gone so far from what she had been, what she had set out to do so many years ago in Honduras. . .

GOING THERE

I

El processo de sensibilizacion empieza por los sentidos, particularmente por los de la vista y el oido… Si al hombre no se le saca de la situacion comoda en que vive, no es possible hacerle ver. (Proaño, Leonidas E., *Concientizacion, Evangelizacion, Politica*)*

The process of becoming sensitized starts with the senses, particularly those of sight and hearing… If a person isn't removed from the comfortable situation that he or she lives in, it isn't possible to make him or her see this.

-1-

Fall 1974

He sat in the Chrysler land cruiser reading. Kevin carried on what seemed to be an endless conversation. Paul wasn't an essential part of this conversation. A grunt now and then seemed adequate to acknowledge that he was there, but just barely. Paul was more interested in his reading than Kevin's incessant blather. He would rather have been alone with his thoughts but since it was easier to hide with his nose in a book, read he did.

"You're not listening to anything I say," Kevin confronted him.

"Sure I am, you were talking about what we would do once we reached Juticalpa," Paul responded.

"Oh, okay, then it's all settled," Kevin stated than launched into another monologue. Paul didn't know what he had just agreed to but figured he'd find out eventually. In the meantime he had ideas of his own for once they reached Honduras.

He had entered Missionhurst as a novice straight out of high school. He wasn't sure exactly why. Some sense of call, some sense of duty. It had been the plan for so long, part of him. Who

6

knows why, he just went. Maybe it was the Missionhurst magazine he had read in seventh grade that had set him on this road. And the sense of excitement that came from the thought of traveling to foreign lands. For whatever reason, he had left his hometown in Michigan, the oldest and only son of proud parents, and went to Washington D.C., missing and yet not missing the turmoil of the late 60's and early 70's as he spent eight years of his life in seminary.

He had spent the first few years of his novitiate attempting to go along with the rules, to modify his own will, sacrificing self to a larger community in order to serve God better through death to self and individuality, standard procedure for religious training. Despite all he or his superiors could do, he continued to grow and mature and become an individual in his own right. The early hours on his knees reciting matins each morning and arduous hours of prayer and reflection had failed to prevent this. Certainly his experiences mixed in with lay men and women at the Catholic University of America in Washington, D.C. proved no great help either in turning out the well-trained, obedient priests of tomorrow for which the school was striving. But Missionhurst Seminary could not be entirely blamed for its lack of success with this one young man. It was the trend around the country those days as more and more brothers and sisters were abandoning their habits and other religious artifacts in a burst of independence and freedom. It was those early post-Vatican II days when everything and anything seemed possible.

And then there was the whole state of the nation at that time, with flower children parading the streets demanding peace and an end to the Vietnam war, blacks demanding equal rights with whites, women demanding equal rights with men, and now religious men and women demanding rights as well – picking up their protest signs and marching in full habit down the streets of Washington, D.C. Was it any wonder that such a time would create such a priest?

His community wasn't to blame. It had done its best to try to submerge that spirit of independence. Blame it all on Vatican II. It was all Pope Paul's fault. Who else could we blame? They turned around the altar and turned the heads of these young priests, brothers and sisters and the Church has yet to recover. Blame it on the Spirit.

Whomever you blame, it was clear that those years at Catholic University of America had no good effect on Paul. There he had made some good friends and even developed relationships with female students. He carried reminders of these friendships in a folder packed away with the load of books he was bringing with him to Honduras. Along with the letters and cards from friends were little sayings and articles he had cut out over his years in seminary and wished to keep close, little bits and pieces of himself from those seminary years, homemade Christmas cards, birthday cards, valentines and going away cards.

After eight years of education and formation in order to fit into a community, Paul had begun to find the restrictions of community life increasingly frustrating. So when in May of 1973 Bishop Nicholas D'Antonio came to Washington in search of priests for his diocese in Olancho, Honduras, Paul saw his chance to escape from the restrictions of seminary and community life and yet still fulfill his desires of being a priest/missionary in a foreign country. He left the restrictions of congregational life with the required reporting constantly to his superiors for whatever he did or wanted and an allowance of twenty dollars per month for any expenses above room and board, to journey to Honduras with Kevin, another dissatisfied member of Missionhurst.

He thought about this as Kevin cheerfully planned out the next fifty years of their lives, assuming that Paul was either already on board, or would jump on board once he was informed.

They arrived in Juticalpa, the capital of Olancho, around one or two o'clock in the morning. Fortunately, they had been in Honduras the previous January and were somewhat familiar with the city and the streets leading to the bishop's house. Paul remembered how he had been struck by both the beauty of the country with its lush tropical trees and flowers but also the extreme poverty.

They pulled up in front of the large darkened two-story box that served as the bishop's house and pulled their bodies loose from the seats of the car where they seemed to have been plastered for so long after so many hours of non-stop driving to finish the final leg of their trip. Since no one was around, they stood in the dim light from the street lamp and tossed stones up at the bishop's window.

"Nick! Nick! Wake up!" they whisper-shouted, not wishing to wake anyone else but not wanting to spend any more time than absolutely necessary from the beds that they expected to be waiting for them inside.

Finally, a light turned on, first in the room they had been tossing stones at, then a little sequence of lights as the plodding steps of the bishop came down the stairs to open the door.

"Welcome," the distinguished gentleman said to the two travel-worn priests and invited them in, always gracious, even at two o'clock in the morning. "You must be tired and hungry after such a long journey."

Bishop Nicholas D'Antonio was well-loved by the priests and religious serving under him. He was known for his love of life and of people, especially the poor of Olancho. In his years as a priest wandering the mountains of Olancho, he was known to have pulled more than four thousand teeth, a skill much appreciated and needed in this country with very few dentists. A native New Yorker, he had been sent to British Columbia after his ordination and then in the late 1940's to Honduras where he had been since then, mostly in the Diocese of Olancho. In the mid-1950's, as a priest, he had brought the Devotion to Fatima to Olancho which proved very popular among the people and eventually led to his being named administrator in 1963 and full bishop in '68, about the time of the Medellin Conference of Latin American Bishops. He came back from the Conference on fire, ready for the establishment of a "new church" – a church committed to the poor and suffering people who were an unavoidable part of daily existence in Honduras.

With this change in direction came new priests, heading in the same direction of work in solidarity with the poor, from both Colombia and France. With this new direction came repression from the government, the rich, those in power and other bishops and members of the church who were not moving in the same direction.

As in other Latin American countries, when the church moved from a church of rich buildings and empty traditions removed from the majority of its people's lives, out into the streets and barrios and campos, there was punishment. The church which had before been with the government, began to be persecuted with the people they had joined. The people in power showed their dissatisfaction with Nick's work in many different ways, including paving the streets of Juticalpa in the early 70's except for the lane in front of the bishop's house and the cathedral.

Bishop D'Antonio received little to no support from the church or his fellow bishops; rather he received criticism. There were few Honduran priests, so the church in Honduras had to rely to a large extent on foreign priests and sisters. As the church would give him no support either by sending priests or money, periodically Nick would have to leave the country looking for both. It was during one such trip that he found the duo that had just turned up on his doorstep.

They exchanged a few words, gave a short account of their trip and the other usual trivialities that social graces required upon arrival at a house for the night. Then they quickly dispensed with the civilities in order to collapse into the only room in the eight-bedroom house that wasn't already filled with visiting priests.

Despite their late arrival, they were up, showered and dressed in time for their eight a.m. breakfast of eggs, beans, tortillas, and coffee – standard fare in Honduras. During breakfast they had a chance to talk with Nick to get an idea of what was going on in the diocese, what their work should be and where they were to go. Paul had wanted to stay in the capitol for a while and study to make up for his lack of language preparation in the states. Then he had hoped to go to Catacamas to work with Ivan Betancour.

Paul had heard a lot already both about Catacamas and Ivan. Ivan was a much loved or much hated priest, depending on whom you asked. A dynamic and charismatic leader, his church and ministry in Catacamas was consequently alive, dynamic and growing. Ivan was a small, fiery Colombian from the proud, independent farmer stock of Antioquia in the western, coffee-growing hills of the country. He had come to Honduras in 1968 to work as a lay person and then returned in 1970 after his ordination to serve with Bishop D'Antonio. Since then his hard work, outspokenness, dedication and devotion to the cause of the poor made him well-loved by the poor and hated by the rich.

Paul had missed meeting Ivan during their visit in January, as Ivan had left to spend some time in Canada, studying marriage preparation courses to supplement the programs he had already started. But Paul had already heard so much about his ministry that he knew that was where he wanted to be. There was a natural division in the diocese between the mountain area and those who worked there, and the valley, which also included some highlands and mountains but not to the extent of the other area. Catacamas was in the valley. Kevin was set on working in the mountains.

Kevin and Paul spent the week visiting different parishes in the area. On Wednesday they drove to San Francisco de la Paz, a town in the mountains, and visited the priest there. Paul wasn't sure how it happened, but somehow during the course of the visit it was determined that this would be their first assignment. By the following Monday they were bumping along the rocky, pit-filled road to San Francisco in their land cruiser.

There were large pot holes all across the dirt road, caused by the strong rains from the mountains. Many of the roads in the north coastal region were impassable, forcing them to take a circuitous route on their way down from the mountains into San Francisco. The area was still experiencing the effects of Hurricane Fifi from earlier that September. Much of the valuable farmland had been flooded. It would take years to recover what they had lost. The only evidence of the hurricane in the central highland region was a few branches and leaves knocked off of trees.

The sky was shining and clear despite the rain earlier that morning. The only evidence that remained was patches of mud in the pot holes which would evaporate by evening in the hot sun. Already the sun had dried out most of the moisture. In the distance a few clouds were forming that could easily bring another tropical downpour from the sky. But for now the sun was high and bright in the sky and the road wasn't quite so sweltering, since a breeze blew through the windows.

Paul appreciated the relief from the constant heat that made all of his shirts cling to him like wet T-shirts after only an hour of wear. And then there was the constant itch exacerbated by the moisture retained by the hairiness of his body. Paul raised a finger and scratched at his bearded face, a habit formed during the last week of the journey to Honduras as the closeness and moisture in the car all the way through Mexico brought out beads of sweat along his hair line and his beard. He passed a hand through his curly scalp of light hair and settled his arm back on the steering wheel.

Rubio–that was how his papers of identification termed his hair, "blanco y rubio, nacionalidad - Norteamericana; Lugar de Nacimiento - Mich., USA; Estado Civil - Soltero; Escribe - Si; Lee- Si; Domicilio - Juticalpa, Olancho; Profecion y Oficicio - Sacerdote Catolico." Profession - priest, how strange that word seemed, sacerdote - priest. He had been ordained for such a short time, it felt awkward, didn't feel like he had earned the title yet.

Customs had taken forever. They had waited in a renovated Shell gas station on the border that had been shot up during the "football" war between El Salvador and Honduras in 1969. The land hungry, packed together peasants of El Salvador had invaded the less densely populated Honduras in hopes of obtaining land. Paul had examined the pock marks in the building from rifle fire, then had sat on the bench against the wall, leaned back and attempted to get some shut-eye, while waiting to get his passport back. Many of the buildings of El Amatillo and other villages along the border bore souvenirs of the constant skirmishes between Honduras and El Salvador.

Paul was relieved when they finally reached San Francisco despite his reluctance to leave Juticalpa so soon and his general displeasure with being assigned to San Francisco rather than Catacamas. The trip, while uneventful, had not been easy. The road they had easily driven the previous Wednesday had been washed out by one of the frequent rainstorms, requiring them to ford the river in their land cruiser.

The rainy season lasted six months, from May to November, with the worst rain in September and October. Except for when violent tropical storms and hurricanes threatened the area, it was a pleasant time to be in Honduras. The rains were cooling and brought new life and lushness to the browning land. Right now the country was luxuriant and green, full of growing vegetation and plants, thanks to the rains. The rain also helped prevent the dust, which was a constant companion other times of the year, from rising into the air. In the interior the temperature was cooler than on the coast or in the big cities. Even if there was rarely a reprieve from the sun, your body adjusted to the even temperatures and wasn't put through the ups and downs and extremes in temperatures experienced by people in countries with four seasons. Here they had two seasons - wet and dry.

Paul glanced around once again at the soon-to-become familiar road leading into San Francisco. Here and there were adobe mud houses, or simple frame, thatch roof houses with children running in and out with the least possible amount of clothing on to provide the most comfort and freedom. Chickens, goats, mules and cows came out at you from all sides of the road, along with men walking, carrying chickens to the market and women toting large bundles or cans for water on their heads. As in most Latin American countries, fifty percent of the population was made up of persons below fourteen years of age, seventy-four percent of the population was undernourished and two thirds lived in poverty.

Paul had been aware of the statistics from his studies, but reading statistics and seeing living statistics were very different. And to actually live the statistics himself was another thing altogether. It's possible to read numbers and say, "too bad, that's unjust," then go on with your newspaper or flick on the TV and forget. It is possible to see the figures, feel the hurt of injustices, but then go home to your apartment or house with only a vague memory of what you had seen and little realization of how what you saw related to the figures. But to live those numbers, be a part of them day in and day out with no escape from the sight of suffering either among other people or in your own home with its cracked adobe walls and lack of running water and electricity – that was another story indeed. It was one that could be momentarily escaped while reading a novel or attending a movie or play, but only momentarily. It was an inherent part of everyday existence here in Latin America.

For the people of the pueblo, the peasant farmers, campesinos, there was rarely any chance for escape. Many of them couldn't read and even if they could, they did not have the time. For the poor, each moment was a harsh reality of life and death, suffering, momentary joys with few chances of escape. For the rich, theirs was a life of constant escape, lived in an unreal world that rarely touched the meaning of life and the depth of the human position. Theirs was a life of escape in TV, movies, sports cars, luxury homes and power. Sixty-seven percent of the cultivable land in Honduras was owned by five percent of the land owners. And these landowners were rarely around to live on the land they owned as they jetted from place to place and inter-married to keep the power in the hands of a few families, the royal elite.

Paul had read the statistics and seen them, but he had yet to live them.

Up and down the volcanic mountains, high plateaus and rolling hills that covered most of the surface area of Honduras were forests of trees, pine and oak, covering sixty percent of the land – one of Honduras' many riches. Of the five tiny countries forming this small belt of Central America, joining Mexico and the USA with South America, Honduras was second in size, although slightly smaller than the state of Pennsylvania. To the north was the Caribbean Sea; east and south was Nicaragua; south, the Gulf of Fonseca; southwest, El Salvador; and on the west, Guatemala. Further south in the Panama Canal zones were the American military bases where most of the Honduran military officers were trained, except of course for those who showed superior intelligence and ability. They were then sent to the states to continue training at U.S. academies such as the U.S. Military Academy in Washington, D.C., a common practice among the military in all of Central America and South America. Take for example, General Somoza of Nicaragua.

The total population of Honduras hardly equaled that of the American city of Los Angeles, although it was second in population of the Central American countries, with Guatemala beating it. Of this population, seventy-six percent lived in the rural areas and twenty-four percent were urban dwellers. As in most Latin American countries, there was an increasingly heavy migration flow to the cities, especially the capitol, creating large barrios, slums, and enormous political, economic and social problems.

There was only one doctor for every 3,464 people nationally. In the rural areas this increased to 15,000 people to one doctor. And there were even fewer nurses and dentists: one nurse for every 8,000 total, one for every 50,000 in the rural areas; and one dentist for every 16,000, and 170,000 to one in the rural areas. Hence, Bishop D'Antonio's record for pulling teeth.

As they rode along and saw the children he wondered, how many would make it to adulthood? How many would learn to read and write? Ten thousand children died annually in Honduras, mostly from intestinal and respiratory disease stemming from lack of water and inadequate sewage disposal, poor food and lack of housing. Ninety percent of the rural population got water from rivers. In urban areas only thirty five percent of the population had running water and only nineteen percent had a sewer system. Fifty percent of the population was illiterate and out of every one hundred children, only fourteen finished fifth grade. The statistics were not promising.

Joan breathed in the moist morning air and surveyed the green expanse around her as they drove through the mountainous terrain, heading for Salama, a small town not too far from San Francisco de la Paz. She, too, was aware of the poverty, lack of heath care, hunger. Who didn't know them? Anyone who had studied the area knew the grim statistics, but for now, for today, she was exhilarated to be so close to starting what she anticipated to be a life-long ministry. The need was great; there was plenty of meaningful work for her to do. In the meantime she was breathing in this new country and all it held for her, the verdant forests, birds, Spanish rolling off the tongues of the smallest children, music to her ears.

Sr. Anita deftly maneuvered their car through the mountain roads, dodging potholes and errant animals and people. They picked up a person or two on the way, villagers that they recognized and that had flagged them down. The sisters were well known in the area. It seemed a terrible waste to drive a car with an empty seat. It was rare that the sisters went anywhere without passengers. This was just how it was done in this country with limited automobiles. The buses were generally filled to overflowing with people and animals. Taxicabs were shared with any number of people that could be squeezed in. And if you happened to be fortunate enough to have a car, you shared it.

Joan shared her seat in the back with a gap-toothed man and his son, on their way back from the capital where they had had some business to take care of. They proved worth their weight when it came time to ford the river. The car was too low to the ground to risk driving through the water, yet to back-track and go to San Francisco by another way would have meant losing a half a day's journey. Pedro talked to some other fellow travelers on the road that saw their predicament. They climbed out of the car to lighten the load, then each man opened one of the four doors and together guided the car across, lifting it just enough to keep the brakes from getting wet. In payment, they all crowded into the car for the remainder of the trip to San Francisco.

It was a relief to drive the way from San Francisco to Salama without any extra passengers. Joan enjoyed the luxury of the back seat all to herself as she prepared to see her new home. She laughed to herself as she reflected back over the past few days and the two young priests she had met and wondered whether their paths would cross. Kevin was by far the more agreeable of the two. Paul had been way too serious, so full of himself and what he was doing, she thought. He needed to lighten up. As if the situation weren't serious enough, why did he have to make it worse?

Kevin had been much more talkative, although he, too, had been full of himself, just in different way. He had been so sure about what he was going to do, how he was going to "help" these poor people. They both could have used a good goose to shake themselves out of their self-importance, she thought.

Finally they pulled into the village and into the lane in front of the simple adobe house that would be home. Several children welcomed them as they pulled into the village, running alongside of the car. Sr. Rosario was a special favorite of the children, hugging each of them and giving them hard candies. Anita was gruff.

"You know you shouldn't encourage them to run alongside of the car. It's too dangerous."

"Si, Anita, I know," Rosario agreed as she smiled at her friends. "Shew, now, go home, vamanos. I'll see you later at church," she told them as she sent them away. "Now let's get you settled," she said to Joan.

It didn't take long for Joan to settle into her small room. There was a single bed with mosquito netting, a desk and chair and a box for storage. No closet or dresser. She neatly folded her clothes into the box, then slid her suitcase and backpack under the bed. Her toiletry items she stashed into the single desk drawer along with her journal. Her books and Bible were left on the top. Then she was ready.

-2-

Kevin and Paul drove the final distance over the mountains and into the valley where San Francisco de la Paz was located. As they pulled up in front of the rectory, a little boy in shorts and a ripped blue shirt approached Kevin's window with his rag and large blackened tin can which served double duty as a footrest for customers to place their foot on while getting a shine and as a container to carry his supplies. Kevin handed him a coin and pointed to his tennis shoes, shaking his head and trying to say something more than "no," in his broken Spanish. Paul didn't even have broken Spanish to rely on so he let Kevin handle the kid and proceeded to chase away a couple mangy mutts who were relieving themselves on their tires.

"Scram . . . damn dogs," he muttered to himself as he rounded the car and joined Kevin who had managed to strike up quite the conversation with the shoe shine boy.

Paul's Spanish may have been lacking, but he knew enough to read the sign posted above the rectory door, "Prohibida la Entrada a Particulares" - Entrance prohibited to particulars. The priest, Alberto Vasquez, was a Spanish Franciscan. It was customary for priests of his order to have this sign posted over the door to their

residence. Paul hated it. Another reason why he had not wanted to
come here, however it had been out of his hands.

The door was opened by the unkempt frumpy little
housekeeper, Sara, who gave them the least welcome she could get
by with and proceeded to walk down the hallway, her shoulders
hunched over, eyes downcast, as she led them to the dining room
where Fr. Alberto was finishing his afternoon meal. Alberto stood
up to greet them and straightway invited them to share his meal.

"I'm sorry, I wasn't sure when you were coming or I would
have waited for you before eating."

"That's quite all right," Kevin assured him. Paul felt his
stomach gurgle. All of that bouncing must have bounced his
breakfast out of him but he thought the best course would be to get
their belongings out of their car before it was broken into and
pounced upon by the urchins across the street playing basketball on
the parish court. Not that there was a lot left or anything of great
value, just clothes and toiletry items. Most of their supplies had
been left that past Wednesday after confirming with Alberto that
they would be staying. These last removed, the land cruiser was
finally free of the heavy cargo it had been carrying for so long. The
frame creaked in relief as the last weights were lifted out of it.

Once their gear was placed in their respective rooms off the
side of the hallway, they proceeded to join Alberto in the dining
room where Sara had silently placed two more plates and more
beans and rice. Paul figured that meant for them to sit down and
eat, so he did.

Alberto was a gracious host despite being a loner, having
lived alone for so long and grown used to his own company. As
were the majority of the religious in this diocese, he was a
Franciscan. Actually Olancho was not officially supposed to be a
diocese at all. Rather it was a prelature which is an area designated
as being under the responsibility of a religious order. In this case
the order was Franciscan. Technically, Bishop D'Antonio wasn't a
bishop because members of religious orders weren't supposed to
have bishops, but he was and they did. From the early seventies on
the Franciscans had been cutting funds to Olancho and pulling out
priests, but so far Alberto remained.

He had entered the seminary at fourteen and seminary life was all he had known. After his ordination he had gone to Peru for several years and then came to Olancho in the early seventies. His ministry in Peru had mostly been alone, visiting people from time to time by boat. In San Francisco he was alone most of the time, except for his housekeeper upon whom he was dependent. He didn't know the first thing about taking care of himself, had never had the training or experience, so at the age of thirty-four he lived much the same life as an old hermit monk, saying his Masses every day and nothing more.

His was a sacramental ministry, often saying anywhere from four to six Masses a day. He had morning and evening Masses, funeral Masses, and every now and then someone would request a novenario, nine consecutive Masses. For each of these Masses he was paid. That was how he kept the parish afloat, from the money he received from saying Masses for people and performing baptisms and weddings. He was given no outside means of support and what little the people could give on Sundays never came close to paying the bills, let alone feeding himself and now two more priests. And so he kept churning out Masses.

Alberto was happy to have someone else to say Masses with him, and was always the gracious host even if he had problems relating to people. When he preached, his voice was a marvel, deep, strong and full. His voice carried across the whole church without the aid of a microphone. In private conversation he toned this down but you could still hear the deep strength under the softer notes.

"Once you are settled in we can talk about the Mass schedule," he said as he showed them to their rooms, then left them as he prepared for yet another round of Masses.

Although Paul wasn't enthusiastic about being here, he figured it could have been worse. He wasn't unhappy and remained undaunted, planning a course of study every morning on his own until he had some mastery of the language. He set his language books and Spanish/English dictionary on the small desk in his room alongside his Bible as a reminder of his intentions. He glanced at the material from MACC, the Mexican American Cultural Center, where he hoped to eventually go and study, but in the meantime he figured he would do the best he could, reading on his own, studying on his own, and basically letting things happen as they may as he struggled with Latin American culture and language. He slid his folder with memorabilia from his seminary years into a drawer.

There were a couple of American sisters in town as well. Kevin and Paul spent a good amount of time with them, being the only other people in the town besides themselves and Alberto with whom they could converse with any semblance of intelligence. And Alberto was questionable as his English was as limited as was their Spanish. The sisters had been there a year and a half. Theirs was mainly a ministry of "presence," they explained. The idea was that simply by their being "present" in this place, praying for the people and the world, something would come of it. They lived in an adequate house and did a lot of visiting. At one point they tried forming a sewing circle and some Bible study groups but that never seemed to catch on.

The people of the town were very friendly and curious about getting to know these two young priests. They took great pains to listen to them and try to understand them but for Paul, his lack of knowledge of Spanish and inability to communicate was extremely frustrating and embarrassing.

Kevin, however, went quickly to work. His limited Spanish was only a small encumbrance. He wasn't afraid of making mistakes and readily attempted to make himself understood. He didn't mind the laughs of the people at his mistakes but laughed himself. Yet he was serious about what he was doing and planned to do. He knew what he was about.

Paul was by nature more hesitant to venture to speak until he had a better grasp of the language. It was like becoming a child again, listening to all these adults standing around you talking at you, about you, and through you, and you could only guess what they were saying and reassure yourself that since they were smiling they were either saying kind things, or making fun of you. In fact it was worse than childhood as even the children put you to shame when these, what appeared to be, little geniuses, rattled off long chains of Spanish words at you and then laughed when you didn't understand. Most of the children had less patience than their parents and enjoyed showing themselves to be smarter than this tall, blond man. Even those who took pity on him and attempted to speak with him got frustrated quickly and returned to their friends with some remark about the dumb Americano.

"¡Hola, Padre! ¿Donde vas?" one boy asked as he walked the streets.

"¿Que?" Paul responded, "What?"

"¿Donde vas?" he repeated as he came alongside him, trying to show with hand gestures what he meant. "¿A la iglesia? ¿El Mercado? ¿Donde? ¿Te puedo ayudar?" He quickly gave up when Paul continued to struggle, laughing as he rejoined his friends. Paul had some hand gestures he would have liked to use himself.

Wherever he went he heard comments about the "rubio Americano," following him. It was a strange experience, this being "different," standing out from everybody else. Even people who didn't know you, knew you, knew who you were, being the only white person in a room full of dark-skinned meztisos, Indians and mulatos. It was an awakening experience to suddenly help you realize how it feels to be on the outside, an alien or alienated person away from the natural supports that you took for granted in your own country.

Here he was marginalized and on the outside because of the language, culture and color barrier. Still he kept trudging along as each new incident sent him back to his textbooks, trying to figure out what had been said to him, while trying to maintain a cool, calm composure befitting an ordained man of God. A week after he first arrived he was asked to do one of the readings at Mass. With no advanced preparation, no warning, without even a chance to read the text over beforehand, he mutilated it. It was a blow to his ego, but he could stand it and was confident that this, too, would pass with time.

Rosa, a friend of Alberto whose husband was a leader in town, introduced Paul to his first real cup of Honduran coffee.

"¿Padre, quieres una cafe?" Paul recognized the word, coffee.

"Si," he replied, hoping it meant what he thought it meant. She poured the brown liquid into a tiny china cup. Paul said no and waved away the teaspoon full of sugar she was preparing to add to the coffee. Paul was surprised by the sweet flavor, finding out later that it had been processed with sugar, but he liked it, which was fortunate. Rarely did he get in and out of a house without first having a small cup of coffee. In Latin America coffee wasn't something served in a large mug that you could warm your hands around and sit with for hours deep in thought or conversation. If you were to drink a standard American sized cup of Honduran coffee, chances are you would be wired all day. The Hondurans usually added a couple spoons of sugar to this already sweetened drink, then tossed it quickly down their throats in a couple of swallows. (The Honduran penchant for sugar was another reason for the pulling of teeth.)

It was also Rosa who got Paul his first piñata for his birthday party, only nine days after arriving in San Francisco. Paul had spent the whole evening with a forced smile on his face as he tried to politely respond to the indecipherable questions and comments that came his way.

"How do you like it here?" Smile.

"What do you think of our country?" Smile.

"How do you like our country?" Smile.

"How do you like our women?" Another smile, at which point everyone burst out laughing.

The rule was, any reason for a party, even if the guest of honor couldn't do more than smile. The Honduran people loved parties and threw them at a moment's notice. It was a primary form of entertainment since only the very rich could afford TV. After the party the little burro piñata found a home in Paul's room in the rectory.

Two weeks after his arrival he took the plunge and said his first Mass in Spanish. He read the whole Mass word for word from the sacramentary and lectionary, the Catholic prayer books for Mass, and even composed a homily which Alberto proof-read for him before reading it word for word from the sheet of paper. Afterwards some of the people came up to him and remarked to him. Paul just smiled, taking all remarks as compliments.

It was sometime during mid-November that he began to realize that if he didn't leave soon to do some studying, he never would. He never went. Paul put the brochures for MACC into a drawer where they no longer taunted him each time he looked in their direction.

Kevin, meanwhile, was feeling some discontent. He knew what he wanted to do, but wasn't sure this was the place for it. He was determined to start an orphanage, maybe another "Boysville" here in Honduras. Certainly there were enough children in need in the area but was there enough support for it? Alberto was too preoccupied with his multiple Masses to be interested, Paul too lost in his studies. The priest in Salama was recently ordained as well and seemed to have the same interests that he had. In fact he had already started the clinic which had been part of Kevin's dream and was interested in opening a home for orphan boys.

As they talked it became clearer to Kevin that this was where God was calling him, not San Francisco. But amidst all of his planning, other plans were being made that they were unaware of that would affect all three of the priests in San Francisco. These plans were being made by the superiors of the Franciscan congregation as part of their general pull-out from Olancho. Certainly three priests were more than any small town warranted. Fr. Alberto was no longer needed there so they were reassigning him to a parish in Tegucilgalpa, the-capital.

Even though they rarely talked, Paul was saddened to hear that Alberto would be leaving. In San Francisco Albert seemed to be making friends and breaking out of his general condition of loneliness. Sure there had been some idle gossip about the young school teachers that visited the rectory but that was just par for the course when you served in church ministry, especially in a small town. It was entertainment. People always had to have someone to talk about. It had seemed to Paul that Alberto was relatively happy here and reluctant to leave, but with Alberto you never knew. He wasn't in the custom of letting people know what was on his mind or in his heart. So he said his farewell at the Christmas Mass and moved on.

And just as Alberto left, Kevin left as well, leaving Paul in charge. If he had felt unprepared to even enter the country, he was even more unprepared to run a parish. He had counted on Kevin's help but Kevin had other ideas.

"Your Spanish is so much better now. You'll be fine. Besides I won't be far away. We can stay in touch. We can still work together," Kevin had said as he left. Paul knew otherwise. He knew Kevin. Once he got started, he wouldn't give a thought to Paul, trying to run a parish by himself with only a rudimentary knowledge of Spanish.

"Besides, I'm sure Nick will send another priest soon, then you can come join me in Salama." Like that was going to happen. Despite his protests, Paul was almost relieved. He had never bought into the idea of starting an orphanage. He had just gone along with it to keep Kevin happy while he figured out what he really wanted to do. He still didn't know what that was just yet, but he would figure it out eventually, that he did know. Meanwhile there was a parish to run.

-3-

The first item on his agenda was to cut out all of the extra Masses, leaving only one evening Mass which actually started on time. It was a rare phenomenon throughout the whole diocese that while everything else in this society started on time, give or take an hour or two, church services started punctually on time, every time. It was a matter of discipline and respect. There were other areas in the peasant's life that required they be on time–work, for example, if they had a job. Certainly the church warranted as much respect as their jobs. So, Paul started Mass and other services on time whether that meant he started with five people present or fifty-five.

Then he added some preparation courses for baptism and marriages, which helped replace some of the income he had lost from cutting out the extra Masses. In his reading and his observations, Paul was leaning more and more towards those members of the diocese who were doing small group organizing and consciousness-raising. None of that was going on in San Francisco so Paul had little chance to observe firsthand what others were doing except by visiting other areas and seeing what the priests and sisters there did and asking them to come to San Francisco to help him get started.

Paul didn't have the command of the Spanish language necessary to teach the baptism or marriage preparation courses, so he had to rely on bringing people in to do them. Finally he was able to travel to Catacamas to meet Ivan Betancourt and observe first hand one of his marriage preparation classes which were so highly acclaimed throughout the diocese.

"Ivan, it's a pleasure to finally meet you," Paul said as he introduced himself after the class. "I've heard a lot about you."

"Don't believe everything you hear, except for the bad stuff. That's usually true," Ivan said with a smile. Paul found the respect he had for this man from hearing about him to be more than justified. In fact his reputation didn't begin to give credit to his dynamic presence among his people, the poor, his compassion and love for them, evoking love from them in turn. As they walked through the city streets he stopped constantly to greet people.

"Fernando, how is your daughter? Has she recovered yet from her fall?"

"Si, Padre, she is much better."

"And your wife?"

"She is so much better thanks to the medicine you brought."

"Good to hear that. I'll stop the next time I'm in the area." He had the same dynamic presence among the rich, only there it was a presence of blatant condemnation which evoked anger and hatred. He loudly condemned the rich landowner and lumber exploiter, Jose Manual Zelaya, to his face in public and on radio programs.

"There is no medicine for the people while Zelaya vacations on the money he exploited from the campesinos," he would say. "Our people are starving while Zelaya cuts down the forests and grows bananas to fatten his belly and the bellies of the owners of the United Brand and Standard Fruit Company."

Paul arranged for Ivan to give the class to the soon-to-be-married campesinos of San Francisco, looking forward to a chance to get to know him better. Paul also invited Enrique Moulin who worked with Ivan in the valley to help him with small group organizing, encouraging peasants to read Scripture and apply it to their own situation. Enrique was also well-loved and well-hated, but not as intensely as Ivan.

Starting in January, Paul set up a fairly regular pattern of staying home in the morning, being available for people to visit, then spending afternoons visiting different communities in the area and homes, sometimes traveling up the mountains to small communities located there, other times remaining in the town. Evenings were basically free, aside from the evening Mass, for study, prayer, perhaps a meeting or just relaxing. Paul did little relaxing as he continued to work feverishly to learn so much, do so much, and yet there was so much he still didn't know.

His visits to different communities always proved an eye-opener. He never once came away from such visits without having learned something or being deeply touched by the simplicity and beauty of these people. He sat in little thatched roof homes of only two rooms, a living room/dining room, and a bedroom shared by two adults and four kids and other relatives. He drank coffee or whatever else they offered him while swatting away flies, both sides struggling to make conversation. Those visits were hard on him, especially the visits with the campesinos higher up in the mountains. It seemed the higher you went, the simpler and less touched by the influences of society were the people. But they were touched by their own culture, their own family groups and superstitions.

The people in the mountains hadn't yet been tainted by the hoarding and acquisitiveness of a capitalist society which would hold on fiercely to whatever it had and search for more, putting the individual above the community. For these campesinos, it was a pleasure, a good, to give. So they gave. Whatever they had, they gave. Be it their last chicken or last bit of coffee, even if it meant their children lived without. They gave with no thought of tomorrow. In some ways, it was a thoughtless giving. How much more difficult giving is to those who have all the worries of tomorrow to chase them, follow them and keep them from giving today.

Paul sat and drank the small cup of ginger tea. He couldn't figure out where this woman had found it. If not ginger tea, it was some kind of spiced tea, quite different from the standard fare of coffee. She must have hauled it out of some secret cache for a special occasion, his visit. The woman offered the small cups, first to him, then to her husband and the other men in the room, moving gracefully about the room holding her serving tray. Her face shone with a gracious smile and shy pride at being able to serve such a rarity. Her limp dress hung loosely over her slim frame, caught at the waste by a long strip of material which doubled as a belt. Her fingers as she reached out with the tray for her husband to take a cup, were long and boney, as were her arms, but those skinny arms hid a tremendous strength which came from years of toting kids and water.

The stamina of these people continuously amazed him. Campesinos would come into town from the hills with a large gash on their hands – swelling up and pussy and in danger of turning green – yet they would say nothing till Paul noticed the hand and said, "as long as you are in town, maybe you should have the doctor look at that."

Paul would run into the same campesino that evening and find that he still hadn't been to the doctor. "I'll go next time," he would say.

They weren't accustomed to running to the doctor with every problem and usually let every cut or blister heal on its own, however painful. It took a lot to faze them. Paul was reminded of a quote by Clement, an early church father: "He (the master) differs from his slaves in one way only, in that he is more delicate and, because of his upbringing, more susceptible to sickness."

An elderly woman entered the hut and received the remaining cup, then took the tray while the first woman went back to her fire to fix some more tea for the men and women waiting outside. They were all curious about the blond-haired padre. Paul didn't have too much to say. After all the introductions and commenting on how good the tea was, there wasn't much else to say. Each time he looked towards someone they just smiled a wide black and white, gap-tooth smile and he smiled back, then stared at the walls. There was a rickety shelf on one wall where the trays and cups had been kept. At various spots about the room were different pictures, cut out of magazines, and snapshots.

Photos, he thought to himself; he should have brought his camera, then he could have taken some pictures rather than try to talk. The campesinos loved to have their picture taken. On one wall was last year's calendar, apparently kept up because of the picture of Our Lady of Guadalupe at the top. On another wall was a "girly" picture of the top half of a nude woman with her arms strategically placed. Paul wondered where they had gotten that one.

"How do you like Honduras, Padre?" the elderly woman asked with a toothless grin.

"I like it very much. It's a very beautiful country." Paul had progressed quite a bit since his birthday party. "I like the mountains and the trees and the people. They are very beautiful."

"Si," the woman smiled in agreement then said something to a man who was leaning against a rickety table in a macho fashion. He responded to her, bringing several cackles from the woman who then smiled back at Paul.

Paul was trying to think of a graceful way to make his exit. He had been abandoned here by a young man from the village that he had gotten to know and who had brought him up into the hills to meet some of his family. He had brought him to this house, introduced him, then went outside. Paul hadn't completely understood what he had said but he figured he was supposed to stay here till he got back. He looked out the open space that served as a door, hoping to spot his guide.

In the doorway was a little Indian boy, maybe three years old. He had been watching Paul the whole time he had been drinking the tea. Paul looked guiltily down at his cup and realized there was none to give him. The elderly woman saw the boy standing in the doorway and called him to her. She gave him what was left of her tea then got up and took the tray around to pick up the empty cups. Paul placed his cup on the tray, stood up and walked self-consciously out the door.

Outside there were several more facsimiles of the child, each of different heights and sex and in various stages of dress, or undress. They stood back and stared shyly at the white stranger that they had suddenly spotted watching them. He stared about at the other huts clustered together and beyond them to the mountains.

There was a beauty in these mountains, a beauty in these mountain people. "I lift my eyes to the hills, from whence shall come my help," Paul thought. Still he could never separate the beauty from the injustice he saw. The campesinos' lack of awareness that there was anything unjust about their situation both frustrated and angered him. In many ways these people were as blind to the injustices in the world and being perpetrated on them, as some of the rich. They didn't see anything wrong with their lifestyle. It was all they had ever known. They didn't know of anything better or want for anything better for they didn't know that it could be different. There was no active discontent with their lives that he could see, only that niggling discontent from some unspoken longing which as long as it remained unspoken, remained only a trifling, sleeping discontent and desire for more, or so he thought.

It is only once the silent unrecognized discontent becomes vocal that the possibility for change arises, the possibility for action, unleashing the anger and frustration locked unrecognized inside them, but also unleashing a potential for hope. It was only as the campesinos came down to the market and saw that the whole world wasn't like them, that not all people had to lug water in cans from the river and other people had medical care for their children and didn't have to watch them die slowly before their eyes, that they began to find words for their discontent.

For so many years the Catholic Church had appeased them in their discontent, encouraging them to accept their lot in life. For years the church had been afraid of unleashing that anger and yet at the same time afraid of hope, afraid of letting people think there might be hope for something better here on earth, rather than hoping for something better when they reach the pie-in-the-sky-after-you-die.

It was much the same for any child brought up in one environment and locked in by that environment, only knowing that one way of life and not realizing that there can be something different from their own experience, that life didn't have to be that way. It's much the same process that helps children break from their parents, break from their past, and create a better place for them and their children, if they are able to make the break and listen to the anger and frustration which is a part of them inside.

It was the air that they breathed, the water they swam in, their culture. Paul remembered this from one of his courses on evangelization in seminary.

"There is a fable," his instructor said, "how a monkey and a fish were in a huge flood. The monkey was able to save itself by grasping a tree branch and pulling itself to safety. Happy and safe, the monkey saw the fish fighting against the current and, moved with compassion by its plight, he bent down to save it. The fish was not happy and bit the monkey's hand whereupon the monkey, angered by the fish's ingratitude, threw it back into the water."

"That's the collision of two different cultures," he had explained. "Culture was the air that he breathed to the monkey, the water the fish swam in. Neither could live in the other's environment. What was safe and inviting to one, was deadly to the other."

Paul certainly could relate to this. He felt like a fish flopping around on land, completely out of his element, trying to learn how to breathe, to convert gills into lungs.

"The monkey thought he was helping the fish, but in reality he was killing it. You need to tread lightly when dealing with another culture. Take time to get to know the culture. Take time to recognize how your own culture has affected you."

Paul was trying, but it wasn't easy. Kevin had taken the same course but had somehow missed this message. Paul tried to understand these mountain people but with little more success than the monkey had had with the fish. Paul was not one to revel in the childlike unawareness of these simple campesinos. Much as he was touched by the simple graciousness and beauty of these people, he couldn't help being frustrated with their lack of awareness. He found himself called to work more with the people in the valley area, in the small towns and cities where there had been more exposure to other life-styles and views, where the discontent was already being brought closer to the surface. In the valley there were already movements to organize the people and raise their consciousness in full operation. There he could be around people already working in these areas and learn from them.

Paul watched the orange yellow beak of a toucan that was jutting out above the leaves of a palm tree. The first woman, the younger one, saw him standing outside of the hut and asked if he would like some more tea.

"No, gracias," he said. She went back behind the hut to her cooking area, pushing the tendrils of hair that had snuck out from under her scarf back into proper confinement.

The littlest of the children had given up staring at this strange man. He ran over to his mother who grabbed him before he could come too close to the fire. She gave him a pat and sent him on his way, calling to his sister to keep an eye on him and telling the other sister to come help her. Still eyeing him, the girl grabbed the three-year-old by the hand and walked off to find a lizard to play with.

Play, what was play? It was not something they knew how to do. The girls helped their mothers around the house, lugging water, tending the fire, tending the younger ones. The boys worked with their fathers on the land, what land there was. Sometimes groups of children would gather to throw stones at a lizard. That was a main source of entertainment. Most often they listlessly drew circles in the dirt till told to do otherwise by their parents or someone else of authority–come eat, come and go to bed, come help me with this, venga aca!

There was a basketball court in front of the church in San Francisco. It gave some of the older boys a form of sport and entertainment. That court was very popular among the boys and young men of the town. Paul often joined them to get a little exercise.

"Why so serious, Padre?" he heard an American voice. He turned and smiled at Sr. Joan.

"Sister, what brings you here?"

"I might better ask you what you are doing so far away from your city in the valley. You forget, this is my territory, up here in the mountains, my people."

"I forget . . . so how is everything in Salama?"

"You should know. There's been quite a bit of change since your buddy Kevin moved in."

"Oh, for the better I hope."

"We'll see. He used that generator that you two lugged from the states to power the church and rectory."

"That's an improvement."

"Might better been put to use to provide electricity to the village," she commented. "And he and Fr. Joe cleaned the church of all of the little statues that were connected with the people's devotions, said it was superstitious claptrap."

"What about the orphanage they wanted to start?"

"Oh, they are starting that all right. You'd be surprised at the number of 'orphans' lining up to leave their homes in hopes of living in a house with the priests, electricity, running water, and three meals a day."

"Is there anything they are doing right in your mind?"

Joan ignored the slight hint of sarcasm in his voice, "At least they brought all those supplies for the clinic. We really needed that, and they've actually been helpful. Kevin knows some first aid. He's been trying to teach others what he knows." She paused, recognizing how negative she had sounded. "I'm sorry. I'm not always so critical. I get this way when I'm frustrated."

Paul waited for her to speak again, rather than asking the obvious question.

"It's just frustrating. They are so sure of themselves and what they are doing. How can they be so sure when they've only been here a few months? How can they be so . . . arrogant. I know they mean well and they are doing good in their own way. It just . . . somehow it bothers me. Like maybe they could have taken a little time to get to know the people first before they started 'solving' all their problems. Maybe it's just sour grapes, because they seem so successful and I'm floundering," she said as she tried to dismiss her qualms. She didn't have the words to explain. Paul was every bit as lost as she. He thought he knew what she was talking about but was having a hard time putting his finger on it enough to put it into words.

"There's a story I heard once, about a monkey and a fish. The monkey thought the fish was drowning so he tried to rescue him," he ventured.

"So, am I the monkey or the fish?"

"Neither. Kevin is the monkey, trying to save the fish. He better watch out or the fish will bite him." Joan laughed at this.

"Would you be interested in maybe helping some at my parish?" Paul went on. "My Spanish is not what it needs to be. I could use someone with your background to help with marriage preparation classes and baptism."

"And what do I know about marriage?" she asked with a smile.

"As much as I do, I bet," he smiled back. "I have someone coming this weekend to teach a marriage prep class. Maybe you could attend and see if it's something you feel you could do."

"Maybe," she said hesitantly. "I'd have to okay it with Sr. Anita and Sr. Rosa."

"It starts at nine on Saturday. Think about it and if you want to come, just show up." Just then Paul saw Eduardo, the young man who had brought him here, walking between the mud houses with another young man.

"Hola, Eduardo, are we leaving soon?" he asked.

"No, Padre, you can't leave yet. We haven't eaten."

"But . . ." Paul began. He did not want to be eating the peasant's food. There could hardly be enough for the family. He protested as Eduardo insisted he stay until dinner was served. Joan smiled as she saw what was happening. She turned to leave as Paul called after her, "Saturday morning, nine. Don't forget." She waved and laughed to herself as she left.

Maybe this would be what she needed, she thought. She was feeling a little lost in her current position. She liked Anita and Rosa but they were pretty busy with their own ministry and had little time for her. She was pretty much on her own which would have been fine if she felt she was doing something worthwhile with her time. Especially since Kevin had moved in. She felt less welcome at the parish. He and Fr. Joe were wrapped up in their plans, which did not include her. She liked the clinic but it was only open two days a week. That wasn't enough to occupy her. She had taken to exploring the country side on a burro and was slowly getting to know people, but with no purpose in mind, no direction. Fr. Kevin and Fr. Joe didn't need her, so maybe she should go where she was needed. It was worth a thought.

Paul reluctantly was led back into the hut where a large platter of beans, rice and chicken and a grainy dry cornbread was waiting on the rickety table. The other men who had been leaning on the table moved so that Paul and Eduardo could sit and eat. Eduardo's sister stood by the table proudly watching the men eat, waiting to see if they enjoyed the meal. Eduardo kept up a conversation with the other men in the room, heaping piles of beans and rice onto his plate, talking with his spoon while shoveling it in. He then picked up a chicken leg and waved it around as he bit off pieces of meat. Paul placed a portion of beans and rice on his plate and a piece of chicken, smiled to the cook to let her know it was good. He finished off with a piece of cornbread. The woman smiled at her daughter who entered carrying glasses of water to offer to the men.

"Oh, no, gracias, yo no tengo sed," Paul politely refused the water, even as the dry cornbread stuck in his throat. He knew better than to drink it. The other girl peered in at the doorway with her little brother waiting for their turn at dinner. Guests always ate first, then the men and then the women and children. To refuse to eat was tantamount to an insult, so Paul took as little as he could get by with without seeming rude.

Eduardo finished his meal, said his goodbyes to the family and was off. Paul smiled his thank you and set off with Eduardo down the road to San Francisco.

Paul wondered, were they as content as they appeared to be, these gracious, smiling people? Paul found it hard to believe that. Even if it didn't bother them, it bothered him. He wanted to do something to alleviate the poverty he saw. Kevin was doing that. The last time he had talked with him he had been so happy about all they were doing. He seemed to be well-liked by the people. He wasn't removed from the people but actively moved among them, greeting them, getting to know them and their families.

If he was a monkey, the people didn't seem to mind. They appreciated what he did for them, or at least so it seemed, but did he ever really listen to them? Did he allow them to change him?

That's what Paul wondered. That seemed to be the missing piece for him. But who was he to talk, how much could he truly listen to the people with his limited Spanish? He felt lost, unsure what to do, how to proceed, like a fish out of water.

Paul remembered another time in the class on evangelization.

"At Christmas, children get presents, right? Let's say you are assigned as pastor to a parish in a village where some are well off and others poor. The poor families aren't able to buy toys for their children at Christmas so you raise money to buy toys which are then distributed to the children at a party. Any problem?" The instructor paused and waited for a response. When no one answered, he continued.

"The fathers of the children were humiliated. Pride is much more important than money, especially in cultures where machismo prevails. So the pastor thinks about it and next Christmas they have volunteers go to the different houses and deliver the toys for the fathers to give to their children. This was better but the fathers were still embarrassed by their lack of ability to buy toys for their children and the toys the children received weren't necessarily the ones they wanted."

"Now, some would say, how ungrateful and quit, but the pastor and members of his committee reflected further on the situation. The next Christmas they gave the money to the fathers so they could buy the toys their children wanted. But there still was a problem."

"What was the problem?" one seminarian asked, "The fathers got to pick out and buy the toys."

"Good question. What do you think? Anyone?"

"What if the fathers used the money for alcohol instead of buying toys?" one person ventured.

"That is a concern, but no, that wasn't the problem."

Finally Paul had responded, "They still had to be given the money rather than having a job so they could earn the money. A job would not only provide money, but pride."

"Correct," he said, "we'll pick up from here next class." Paul wondered again what Kevin had been doing during this class.

Paul wondered about the many statues and the devotions associated with them in his own church. Should he get rid of them too? It was a carryover from early Indian religions and superstitions. With the arrival of the Catholic missionaries years ago, many of their gods had been acculturated, intermixed with the saints of the church. It was a way for them to hold onto their old beliefs while accepting the beliefs of these white men; a way to put a Christian face on a pagan religion, and in the process transform them. They had put Christianity into a language they could accept and understand. Some felt it was not only harmless, but important in reaching out to the indigenous people on their terms and in ways they could understand. Others felt it was a perversion of the faith. Paul was trying to tread lightly.

Devotion to the saints was very strong. Devotion to Mary, especially in the form of Our Lady of Suyapa, patroness of Honduras, was exceptionally strong. The story told is that on a Saturday in January in 1747, Alejandro Colindres and Lorenzo Martinez, an eight-year-old boy, were returning to the village of Suyapa, tired from working all day gathering corn. They were half way there when night fell and they laid down on the hard ground. Right away Alejandro felt that something, apparently a stone, was preventing his finding a comfortable position for his back. In the dark, he picked it up and threw it far away.

On lying down again he felt the same discomfort, but this time he did not throw it, instead putting it away in his knapsack. At day break he discovered that the mysterious object was a small image of Our Lady carved in cedar wood. The carving measured only six and a half centimeters, but was a source of great devotion to the Honduran people.

Much of their religious faith had become tied up in the visible form of statues. Some of the people had little concept of a God beyond these statues, so in some ways maybe Kevin and Joe were right in their actions.

Paul came back from the mountains with much to think about. So much suffering, so much injustice, but what was he to do?

Paul got rid of Sara as soon as Fr. Alberto had left. He was tired of finding hairs in his food from her unkempt head and eating mushy rice and scorched beans, besides having to frisk her every night before she left (not a pleasant occupation given the state of her body) to make sure she wasn't walking off with tomorrow's dinner. Sara had stood as though not understanding, feigning ignorance, as Paul told her she was fired. It took some time but finally he made himself understood. Afterwards he quietly put some beans on his burnt tortilla as he figured out what to do next.

He made arrangements with another woman in town to provide one meal a day. The rest he figured he could take care of himself. That was how Nunilla, arch enemy of Rosa de Peralta, became a part of his household, straining his relationship with Rosa. Both Nunilla and Rosa came from the more affluent sector of town. Nunilla's brother was the head of the hospital and quite well off. Paul wasn't sure why she bothered with the job at all, except maybe to make Rosa jealous. He also didn't know why he had hired her, especially since half the time she didn't show up. Still his range of acquaintances was very limited so he took whom he could find and put up with the rest.

Where Sara had been unkempt, her hair flying everywhere, Nunilla was always very proper, her greying hair tied firmly in a bun and clothed in spotless, white dresses. She also spoke to him, something Sara rarely had done. It was a nice change.

Along with the other new experiences and sights Paul was being exposed to on a daily basis, was the physical violence which seemed as much a part of everyday existence as the suffering. None of the basic questions of life and human nature were covered over in this barren yet beautiful country. Physical violence, political turmoil, cruelty to people by others, and exploitation of people was a blatant part of the country. It was unlike middle class America, where violence is covered with fancy phrases and manipulative natures disguised behind false exteriors, hidden even from people themselves.

Paul didn't think he would ever get used to so many guns. Everywhere. Not just in the hands of the military, but in the hands of anyone who could afford one. They used them when they could, often taking the law into their own hands. It was the law of the gun which at times made Paul feel he had been transported back into the days of the Wild West and the Westerns he had read as a child. He expected at any time to be challenged to a shoot-out or to be told to get out of town before sundown. It put you on edge, waiting for something to happen. Machetes, too, hanging down the length of the campesinos' pants, were everywhere.

He hoped he never got used to such sights just as he hoped he never got so used to the sight of children running naked in the streets with bloated bellies and pock marks that he could turn a blind eye to them. Or beggars, crippled and sitting in front of the market place, tugging on your pant leg, asking with open palms for something to eat. Or mangy, starving dogs rooting in the garbage in the streets and careworn women carrying a child in one hand and a can of water on their head, cooking over an open fire where children could and did tumble in the minute the fire was left untended.

He hoped he never got used to the sight of scarred children who had lost or mutilated a limb in a fire. Or the gaping grins of so many of the adults who lacked any proper dental care and loved their sweets. He hoped never to get so used to these sights that they failed to move him, touch him, and push him to work for something better. He hoped never to get used to the sight of guns as an ordinary part of life. He hoped always to work for a time when they were not a part of anyone's life, when the houses and signs speckled with bullet holes were the only reminders of a time gone by.

So, in late March when he heard that there was some shooting going on in a town just up the road near the school that many of the children of San Francisco attended, he reacted immediately in fear for the lives of the children without pausing to check further into the situation. He rushed, Lone Ranger-like, into the town to rescue the children – only he rode into town on a bus and not a horse.

"The children, we have to get the children. In the school, they are in danger." He pointed in the direction of the school repeating, niños, la escuela, peligro! Children, school, danger.

He couldn't understand why no one else was concerned. He ran from place to place trying to find someone to help him but everywhere he received the same complacent looks in return for his wild gesticulations which he had hoped would make his Spanish more understandable.

The owner of the bus finally threw up his hands and rattled off something to one of the drivers, telling him to go with the padre. They climbed in the bus and drove off in search of the children.

A friend of the owner stretched from where he had been leaning against the adobe wall and questioned him, "What is wrong with the padre?"

Pedro shrugged his shoulders and said, "Loco," shaking his head. Then they started up their conversation again.

By the time the bus arrived, any danger the kids might have been in was over. There had been a shooting but nowhere near the school and as far as he could tell no one had been hurt. Random shots had been fired in a conflict but no one was hurt. It had been a sign of bravado and machismo.

Paul loaded the children on the bus and brought them home anyway. The kids enjoyed the novelty of the ride. Paul didn't enjoy the bill that was handed him upon return of the bus. Paul was still too upset about the whole incident to feel embarrassed. In fact, it was only later that he realized, much to his own embarrassment, that maybe he had been wrong after all. He had rushed into something he knew little about like a paternal savior, rather than allowing them to handle their own problems.

Despite what he said about a paternalistic church that treated adults like children, he had fallen into the same trap. It was so much easier to rush in and save someone than to help them save themselves. So much easier to tell others what they should do than to trust them with free will. Easier to give charity, be the savior and enjoy the quick rewards from having done something, than to struggle with the deeper questions. One was the way of charity, the other of liberation. As he struggled to learn the language, he often felt like a helpless child. Here he was, treating these campesinos as helpless children rather than as the grown men and women they were.

His first chance to see the damage guns could do was that
May. He was attending a course taught by Enrique Moulin in
Gaurizama, a pueblo to the northwest of San Francisco. Joan had
attended the course with him. She had accepted his request to help
out, had attended the classes that had already been scheduled and
had tentatively started holding her own. Every other week or so she
would come to San Francisco and stay with the sisters there while
teaching her classes. The sisters were kind and welcoming, warmly
taking her into their home even though Paul had fallen out of favor
with them because of his continued interest in "those priests" – the
ones organizing among the poor of the country.

Joan shared little of what she was learning and doing, lest she,
too, fall out of favor. Rather she talked about her work at the clinic
and among the children and her journeys up the mountains. She
had become a common sight in the mountain region, riding daily to
visit families, bringing her first aid kit. Slowly, Joan felt she was
finding her place, getting a toehold among the people as they
began to trust her. This was combined with the propaganda she
was getting from Paul and the priests he brought in. She took it all
in and let it rest inside her mind, not sure what she would do with
all of it, but somehow sure that it would become clear over time.
She was preparing herself for something. She wasn't sure what, but
she was confident she would know it when it came along.

Class had hardly begun when someone came running in
saying a kid had been killed and they needed someone to bring
back the body. That ended the course. Paul had insisted that Joan
wait for him there.

Paul rode the distance with Enrique and the others on
horseback, his sandaled feet slipping out of the stirrups constantly.
The kid was sixteen or seventeen. It had been a case of personal
vengeance, someone taking the law into their own hands. What
could someone so young do to warrant such a death? But whoever
had money and arms, ruled the law. Few of the large landowners in
Olancho actually had legal titles to their land. But they had money
and guns and that was title enough.

The boy had been shot four or five times. Little patches of red
showed where the bullets had entered. That wasn't bad. That he
could handle. Paul stared at the body as several men flipped him

on his side, getting ready to lift him and carry him back in procession. That was it. That was the sight that remained in his head for hours, days, weeks, afterwards. The whole back of his head had been macheted to a pulp of red, leaving a large splotch of crimson on the ground and dripping out more blood and brains except for the few spots where the blood had started to coagulate, forming black splotches around the edges of the skull that remained. The stench mixed with the hot air and flies quickly appeared to settle on the fresh blood. Paul could feel the muscles of his stomach begin to retch, but he wouldn't let himself heave and simply passed his hand through his hair and over his face and turned away.

They walked back in procession with the women, not crying, but wailing in an unnatural, inhuman manner, gnashing their teeth which produced a sound that was hard to shake from between his ears and stayed with him long after he left the town.

When Joan saw his face, she quietly said, "You want me to drive home?"

Without saying a word, he handed her his car keys. They drove back in silence with the exception of when he told her to pull over the car and then got out. She could hear the sound of vomiting then he came back.

"You okay?" she asked tentatively.

"Yeah, just keep driving," he mumbled.

-5-

Paul was getting some firsthand information about big business, the multi-nationals and corruption in governments, through the newspaper articles he read each day. The banana companies were very much the controlling factors in the country, determining the economy and controlling the government purse strings. Currently the papers were reporting the scandal of the bribe offered by United Brands of Boston, a multinational company known as the "octopus" in Honduras because of the way it had its tentacles everywhere and was sucking and squeezing the life out of the country.

Then there were the reports of General Lopez Arellano, head of the government who was ousted and replaced by another general, General Melgar. It had been time anyway, time for another political overthrow. Since Honduras had received its independence from Spain in 1838 there had been over 135 revolutions, sometimes two or more in the same year. They had been due for one.

The history of the banana companies in Honduras has been a long one. Since 1870 there has been unlimited exploitation by the two banana companies, United Brands and Standard Fruit, a branch of Castle and Cooke, Inc. These two companies accounted for one half of the agricultural output of the country; for about thirty five percent of the nation's total exports; and for twenty percent of the national income. They also had 120,000 acres of the best land in Honduras, ten percent of which was used for agriculture, twenty five percent for cattle and sixty five percent of which lay unused.

Thanks to United Brand's extremely poor working conditions on their banana plantations, eventually a militant labor movement grew, producing a high degree of political organization in its peasant unions, something lacking in most other Central American countries. The companies reacted to the union by employing armed thugs to intimidate striking workers and kidnap union leaders, flying them to neighboring El Salvador and dumping them. They also hired thugs to machete small growers' banana shipments as they lay on railroad platforms. Workers were paid seventy-five cents a day and received no benefits, no vacation, no medical care, and no redress for arbitrary dismissal.

These conditions led to the strike of 1954. The strike lasted seventy days despite deaths and arrests of union leaders. Throughout the seventy days peasants from all over the country supported the workers, sharing their small portions of beans and bananas. Due to their show of solidarity, the banana workers then helped the peasants organize into unions, which strengthened both the worker and the campesino movements in the country.

When Honduras and six other countries in Latin America attempted to join together and form their own OPEC of banana-producing countries, they decided to impose a tax of fifty cents on each forty-pound box of bananas shipped out of the country to offset spiraling transportation and fertilizer prices. The banana companies were outraged. Standard Fruit threatened violence to the governments involved. United Brands took a quieter tack and bribed the Honduran government to half the tax for $2.5 million annually; then, in turn it took advantage of the tax to raise the price of bananas sold to the U.S. by fifty cents a box, increasing their profits by an even larger margin.

Details of the bribe came to light when Eli M. Black, chairman of United Brands, jumped from his Manhattan office window to his death forty four floors below. Black's suicide blew the whole scandal of "bananagate" wide open and Oswaldo Lopez Arellano was forced to resign after he refused to allow a government commission to examine his foreign bank account.

Arellano had taken power through two military coups. His was a mildly reformist government and did do a few good things, as typical of many reform leaders in Latin America. He did just enough to keep the people down, keep them hoping things were changing, getting better. He initiated land reform programs that kept them hoping that they may be one of the lucky few who actually received land.

When General Melgar took over, even what little reform had been done was stopped and curtailed. This led to a lot of agitation among the campesinos and added to the tensions that usually began to build up each April and May, during planting season. Then the peasants had to choose between eating and buying seed to plant. Different demonstrations started and peasants would seize land as a protest and occupy land that wasn't being used.

In the meantime the landowners and military were looking for a chance to do something to stop the growing protests. They got their chance.

Forgetting the massacre of six peasants in Olancho in 1972 at Talanquera, the Christian Democrats National Union of peasants organized a "March on Hunger" as a protest against the government's failure to follow through on its promise for land reform. Many observers were opposed to the march, for they felt the timing was bad. However, plans continued and the march was set for June, starting at Olancho the morning of June 25th at 2a.m.

with a Mass lead by Enrique Moulin in the grassy area outside of the peasant center.

After the events of the past month, Paul and Joan were looking forward to their vacation in Tegucigalpa, the capital of Honduras. Paul's sister, Susan, was coming for a visit and Paul was looking forward to having some time with her. They left on June 24th. Once again they had plowed through the river where the road had been washed out last October and was yet to be fixed. Spirits were high as they pulled into the capital. It was only through word of mouth, radio, and various reports that Paul and the rest learned through a slow, hard process lasting several months what actually had taken place on the 25th that caused them to have to spend the summer exiled in the capital.

GOING DEEPER

II

El cambio de mentalidad es una transformacion profunda. No sola es edquisicion de ideas: es cambio del ser, cambio del corazon, conversion. En determinados circulos de personas, se puede oir hablar de una palabra deconocida: metanoia . . . (Proaño)*

The change of mentality is a profound transformation. Not only is it acquiring ideas: it is a change of being, change of heart, conversion. In determined circles of people, one can hear talk of a little known word: metanoia . . .

-6-

Someone was crying, sobbing. She had to get up to help, but she couldn't. Her body wouldn't move. She was paralyzed. Then she woke up, the sound of sobs still ringing in her ears. Slowly she moved her hands, wriggled her toes, willed herself into consciousness. She could move after all. It had just been a dream. But who had that been, sobbing so desperately? Dave was still asleep. He hadn't heard it. Had it been a dream as well, this voice, sobbing in her right ear, inside her head?

She looked at the clock. Four o'clock. It was too soon to get up, yet too late to go back to sleep. She'd just get back to sleep in time to be awoken. She knew this from past experience. She could lie in bed and toss and turn until six, or get up and start her day. She chose the latter.

The bed creaked as she lifted her weight out of it. Dave turned over.

"Is everything all right?" he mumbled.

"Go back to sleep. It's too early to get up," she told him.

Dave obediently turned back over and went to sleep. Chances were he hadn't even heard her in his sleep-induced haze. He wouldn't even remember when he woke up later.

She put on her bathrobe and walked stiffly down the stairs and into the kitchen. The coffee pot was exceedingly slow as she watched with coffee cup clutched in her hands. She stared out at the snowy landscape. How had she gotten here? How indeed? Who was it that had been crying? Who had awoken her from her deep sleep?

Joan dug out the box with the mementos from her years in Honduras, carried it to the kitchen table and pored over it as she drank her coffee. Pictures of children, always children, they were everywhere and loved to have their picture taken, as did their older relatives and friends, parents, grandparents, aunts, uncles, cousins. Joan was never at a loss for a subject. In fact, at times she pretended to take pictures after she had run out of film. There she was, next to that burro of hers, surrounded by kids. How young she looked. How happy. How had she managed to be so happy with all of the poverty, and yet she had been happy, maybe the happiest in her life. She felt some guilt at that thought. After all, her life included all the years of her marriage and raising her children. She had been happy then. She loved her husband and her sons, loved being a mom, but it was a different happy. She had been happy in Honduras, despite everything.

She looked through all of the newspaper clippings she had saved:

"HONDURAS ARRESTS FIVE IN
DISAPPEARANCE OF TWO PRIESTS,"
The Miami Herald, Saturday, July 12, 1975.
TEGUCIGALPA, Honduras.

"INQUIRY IN HONDURAS UNCOVERS DEATH
OF SEVEN AFTER PROTEST CLASH,"
New York Times, Friday, July 18, 1975.
TEGUCIGALPA, Honduras

"MISTAKEN IDENTITY HINTED," July 18, 1975,
MILWAUKEE - The family of the Rev. Michael
Jerome Cypher, whose body was found today in
Honduras, believe that his death may have been the
result of mistaken identity.

"HONDURAS CHARGES OFFICERS IN
KILLING," The Washington Post,
Thursday, July 24, 1975, TEGUCIGALPA.

"KILLINGS STALL PEASANT REVOLT,"
The Washington Post, Monday, July 28, 1975.

It brought back so many memories, memories of those two
and a half months spent in Tegucigalpa, trying to piece together
what had happened in Olancho, what had happened to their brother
and sister, priest and religious in the area. Waiting as some showed
up, finally, others didn't. The clippings told of peasant revolt,
longstanding disputes over land, as background to what had
happened.

It seemed that a planned attack on the church in Olancho had
occurred. She remembered that meeting on June 28 in the
archbishop's home. The bishops of Honduras, priest and religious
had all gathered to hear of a plan that had been discovered against
the church. Bishop Nick had not been present. He had been out of
the country at the time of attack, a fortunate circumstance since it
was later discovered that his name had been among the names
targeted, with a $10,000 price on his head. She read over the sheet
with instructions on how to deal with the clergy.

*Do not attack the Church as an institution and never the
bishops as a group, but attack only in one section or part
where the Church is most advanced and progressive.*

*Above all attack the foreign clergy. Show insistently that
these are responsible for preaching armed warfare and are
linked with international communism and that these have been
sent for the exclusive purpose of moving the Church toward
communism.*

Open a special file on all priests and religious and also on certain bishops and religious orders.

At the beginning do not bother religious houses because this would cause unfavorable publicity. Of the priests on the list, arrest them in the country or on the street, preferably in places where there aren't many people present.

Once the arrest is made, insert among their papers or in their rooms subversive propaganda and some type of arm and have this ready to discredit them with the bishop and in public opinion.

This had explained the pictures in the daily papers showing rifles, pistols and subversive literature supposedly found in the homes of those priests and religious who had been arrested. She didn't remember the source of the instructions, smelled of CIA though. It had been a difficult time. Daily word of persecution and violence filtered into the capitol. The landowners and government officials terrorized the people. People were arrested. The government blamed the landowners, the landowners blamed the church.

"Local and foreign Communists are responsible for the whole thing," a leader of the ranchers stated. "They turned the have-nots against the haves. We have full information that they're Communists . . . or leftists, or extremists or whatever you want to call them. What I know about for sure are the sermons I've heard the foreign padres preach for years on the radio, those sermons preached class hatred." They heard this and other statements like it broadcast over the air waves.

The church pressed for information about the whereabouts of the missing priests and religious. Slowly word came back, who was alive, who wasn't. Fr. Michael Cypher, an innocent bystander who happened to be in the wrong place at the wrong time, had been mistaken for another priest who had worked with the peasant union and died in his place. Fr. Ivan Betancourt, well known for his stand with the peasants and against the landowners was among the dead, along with others.

It took a while for the exact numbers to come out. Arrests of suspects were made after church authorities threatened to organize massive protests. Once five were arrested, three army personnel and two landowners, two thousand university students had staged a "silent march" to the presidential palace to demand punishment of those arrested. The government insisted those in the military had acted alone. The government, landowners and church continued to point fingers, trying to sort out what had happened.

Frightened by the continual presence of soldiers, there was no freedom of movement, no freedom of speech in Olancho. With no official church presence, a few brave lay leaders continued to gather and pray together, risking their lives.

Making this time even more difficult was the lack of support from the official Church. Hopes that had been high at the time of their meeting at the archbishop's home, had been squelched as the archbishop and other bishops had opted for silence in the face of the persecution of the Church in Olancho. Despite official statements made to newspapers they had chosen the course of least resistance, hoping for a quiet resolution to the problems in Olancho by letting the military and government deal with the situation. The exiled priests and religious of Olancho had felt like they were a problem to be dealt with, rather than brothers and sisters in Christ, working for the good of the people.

Joan had stayed at the house in Tegucigalpa that she had remembered in her dreams. It had been a relief, being away from Salama and San Francisco, a needed break from the intensity of the poverty. Yes, there was poverty in Tegucigalpa as well, but the house she was staying in was enough removed from it that she could avoid it with effort. She could stay inside the cool, clear, clean walls of the house, rock in a rocking chair and take it all in. She went over in her head all the events of the past eight months. She sorted through it and allowed herself time to heal in order to be ready for when it was time to return.

But she couldn't escape all of it, as her heart remained with the people and ached at the news of violence. She feared for the families she had left behind, wondered how they were faring amid the bloodshed. Part of the frustration of being exiled was the lack of activity. While she had welcomed the quiet at first, as weeks became months, she became increasingly restless at the inactivity. It was hard to know what to do when at any time she could be called back to Olancho. She didn't want to start something that would have to be abandoned.

She visited priests and sisters that were working in the slums of Tegucigalpa. Funny how all slums looked alike, she thought. It was not so different from the slums of Lima, Peru, where she had spent two months one summer, living with two other sisters in a one-room shack with just a bare light hanging from the ceiling for light, when they had electricity that was more often off than on. It had been so grey, a world of grey, cloudy skies, dirt and dust covering everything. The only relief from the grey had been the trip they had taken into the mountains. Finally the sun had burst through exposing blue sky.

The poverty had been less oppressive out in the colorful rain forests. That was why she had opted for work in a rural area rather than a big city. The unrelenting intensity of overcrowding, dirt, squalor, and the theft that was part of slum life was too much for her. She was happy to retreat back into the house provided for her with the other sisters after her visits to the slums and await word for when she could return to the rural area of Olancho. As she waited she made her plans.

Not so for Paul. He couldn't rest, was constantly trying to find out what had happened, kept agitating to get back to Olancho. He spent his time in meetings with other religious stranded in the capital and reading the local paper, listening to the radio. They had little else to do besides meet, talk, make plans – plans that they would not be able to implement until they knew what was going on.

Paul's sister had come to visit and found herself trapped in the city as no one was allowed to leave or go anywhere. It wasn't much of a vacation for her as Paul was reluctant to go anywhere or do any of the usual activities tourists do lest he somehow miss out on a vital piece of information or miss out on some important planning. He felt guilty for any minute not focused on what was happening in Olancho. Now and then Joan and Susan were able to reluctantly drag him away from the radio and his meetings to visit a museum or to go out for a meal. He was always anxious to get back.

Once Susan made it home, she and her parents had begged Paul to come back for a while.

"You can't do anything there. Why not come home? You can come back when you can get back into Olancho," they said, but Paul was afraid that once he left the country he would not be allowed back in, as had happened to other priests and religious. Kevin had no such qualms, spending the two months back at the states, soliciting funds for his charity work. Paul anxiously paced about his room, "How could he leave during a time of crisis," he had thought. "We need to be here in solidarity with our people."

He spent the time thinking about what had happened. He didn't know what he had expected when he had come. He had tried to not have any expectations, but he hadn't expected this, hadn't expected so much violence and certainly not directed at the church. He was beginning to realize that being here with these people, was more than just spreading the faith that he had grown up with. He needed to develop a new faith, somehow related to his childhood faith, yet new. His faith, his concept of God, religion and Christianity didn't work here. It wasn't America, wasn't the same culture, wasn't the same God. He prayed to an American God but that God didn't exist for the people of Honduras. Theirs was a different God coming out of and reflecting their culture. His God reflected his American upbringing, his family life, his culture. His God didn't fit here in Honduras, was not, could not be real to these people.

If he was to work with these people he had to discover a new God, their God, a God who had meaning in a third world country, a Jesus who spoke to their lives every day and was real to them. He had to discover a God to whom they could relate. He had to learn a new way to pray, in Spanish, with the subtle differences that a change in language brought, and more important, in Honduran Spanish which brought in all the differences of a different culture. It was a different language from Spain's Spanish. He was the stranger in a strange land and he had to make their God, his God, too.

He couldn't wait to get back, but not to San Francisco; finally Paul was going to get his wish to go to Catacamas to minister where Ivan Betancourt had ministered. Kevin had thought him crazy, couldn't understand why he wanted to leave San Francisco.

"Look at all you could do. We could help you open up an orphanage there as well. We could work together. Why go somewhere where you don't know anyone?" But Paul remained resolute in his plans.

He called Bishop Nick once it was safe for him to come back into the country so he could be with his priests and sisters in the capital. In mid-September they finally got the okay from the government but rather than everybody rushing back their own separate ways, it was decided that two groups would go back for a month then report back. Then they would discuss the situation and finalize plans. Paul was to be part of one group along with another priest and two sisters.

-7-

Fall 1975

After two and a half months stuck in the capital, in a state of limbo, not knowing what was going to happen next, not knowing if any of them would be able to return to Olancho to work, they finally returned. Slowly the information as to what had happened on that fateful day in June became clear.

It had begun at two in the morning, June 25th, in Juticalpa with a Mass out on the grassy lawn inside the February 18 Peasant Training Center. After the Mass those who were walking began their march, carrying with them the torches that had been used to light the Mass, while the people who stayed behind went into the three-story building that was the center to keep vigil. The center had originally been a Catholic school but had since been turned over to the peasants. Different people were assigned to drive cars with food to the walkers at various stages along the journey. By the time they reached Tegucigalpa they were hoping to have the original number of nine hundred marchers increase to 12,000 as peasants from different villages along the road joined them.

At about eight that morning, the peasants inside the center were disturbed by someone banging on the door followed by the sound of shots. Several people ran to the windows to see what the problem was and were met by the sight of a group of school children chanting that they wanted their school back. In front of the group, banging on the door and demanding that they open it, was the superintendent of schools. He had led the group, instructing them as to what they should say and how they should behave.

Overhead was the sound of a military plane going by as a group of local police and soldiers marched past the children and broke into the building, riddling the peasants with gun fire, killing five peasants and wounding two others. They then went among the ranks of the scattered peasants and pulled out certain leaders of the peasant organizations to take with them to prison.

Fr. Michael Jerome Cypher was in town that day seeking medical care for a peasant from his village. Cypher was an American, Franciscan Friar. He had only last December returned to Honduras after a stay at his home in Medford, Wisconsin, due to an illness from an insect bite. He was still struggling to make inroads in the Spanish language and knew nothing about the events of that morning, of the March on Hunger, or any kind of peasant movement. He stood in amazement in front of the riddled building. Seeing an injured man he was preparing to come to his aid when he was grabbed by the police.

"Get him. He's one of those priests."

Fr. Cypher, or Fr. Casimiro as he was called by the peasants, his Franciscan name, was grabbed by two men and found himself facing a rifle as a rapid fire of questions were shot at him. He struggled to understand what was happening and the questions.

"I'm Fr. Casimiro," he answered the barrage. He assumed one of the questions must have been what was his name. "I'm a Catholic priest," he added, guessing that that had been another question among the many. One of the men threw him up against the wall and frisked him for any weapons and papers of identity. He pulled out the father's billfold with his American driver's license and showed it to one of his superiors.

"He says his name is Casimiro, but here it says Michael J. Cyphers." The Sargent looked carefully at the license. They were looking for a Father Michel who worked closely with the peasant unions at the center. "He must be the one." He approached Michael. "Give me the keys to the institute," he demanded.

Fr. Casimiro was taken aback by the question. "What institute?" he asked. He was only vaguely aware that such a place existed.

"You know which one. The Peasant Training Institute where you work."

"But I don't work at a peasant training center . . ." Casimiro was cut off by a knee to the groin which doubled him over in pain.

"Take care of him," the Sargent ordered, "put him with the rest." The men then beat him and put him in jail with the five other prisoners they had taken from the center.

The peasants who were marching were stopped just as they reached the highway to Tegucigalpa by a large ditch dug along the road in front of them and several cars full of military who drove some of the people back but for the most part sent them back, walking, on the same road they had just traveled, this time in defeat.

"Bye, Mama. I'll meet you tomorrow at the airport, okay?"

"Si. Goodbye, my son. Have a safe journey and take care of Maria Elena." The grey haired lady proceeded to give her son, her future daughter-in-law and the other young woman who was going to be riding with them, kisses of farewell before they climbed in the car to start the journey to Olancho. Ivan had deemed several hours in a car as much too long for his aging mother. But as he wished to show his prospective sister-in-law some of the countryside, he had decided to drive her to Olancho, along with a university student, Ruth Garcia, and then pick up his mother at the airport in Juticalpa the next day. His mother had just flown-in from Colombia with Maria Elena to visit with her son. Maria Elena was to marry Ivan's brother, Bernardo, that December.

As they drove through Campamento, someone recognized Ivan and stopped him to warn him about what was happening in Juticalpa. Up till then Ivan had had no notice about the situation.

"I have to go. My mother will be arriving at Juticalpa tomorrow and I have to be there to pick her up," Ivan stated and undaunted continued on his way, continuing his guided tour, filling Maria Elena in on everything there was to know about his beloved country and the people of Honduras.

A sense of terror was spreading throughout Juticalpa. The military patrolled the streets of the city after the arrest of the five peasants and one priest and the ransacking of the center. That night they rounded up all the priests and sisters in the town, plundering each convent and rectory, and put them in jail.

At about ten-thirty that night, the six bound prisoners from the morning were thrown in the back of a pick-up truck which then joined with a convoy led by Major Jose Chinchilla and drove to the ranch, Los Horcones, owned by Jose Manual Zelaya. The trip had been long and hard, laying in the back of the truck and feeling every bump of the rocky, rutted dirt roads. Fr. Cypher had heard a certain amount of conversation at first as the truck had joined up with Chinchilla, then had been the unending stretch of time as they bounced along the road.

Michael could hear that they were not alone. There were other vehicles and now and then words would be shouted back and forth, but for the most part they rode in silence except for the moans of his fellow riders in the back of the truck. No words of comfort could be spoken as any attempt to speak was met by a rifle butt being jabbed in their back. The peasants and priest rode silently on, the priest praying to his God whom he knew had to be somewhere nearby. If only he would rescue him from this mess, rescue the others with him.

Michael held firm in his belief that God was still there and would somehow help him through this awful night. If only he knew what he was being accused of, knew why he was being treated like this, then maybe he could defend himself. But he didn't know what was going on, didn't know why he was out here on the lonely road with five other men, bound and gagged and sharing something in common, sharing their common suffering.

He thought of his family in Wisconsin, his mother, what this would do to her if she knew what was happening to her son at this moment. Even with nine brothers and three sisters, he knew she felt the wounds of each one of her children as intensely as if there had only been one. He felt close to his mother, close to her right now, and didn't want her to suffer over him. He vowed that he would never tell her about the events of the day and night. He would never burden her with it.

There was so much to think about during the long journey, during the stay in jail. The peasants' thoughts ran to their loved ones. Their wives and children, their parents, would they see them again? Who would take care of their families if something happened to them? What were they suffering now? Sometimes they wanted to curse the union, curse themselves for their involvement in organizing their neighbors to resist and demand their rights, curse themselves for what would happen to their children now. They were doing this for their families, for their children, for their friends and neighbors so that life could be better for them. What good was their work now, now they may no longer be around to carry on the fight? And they couldn't even offer muffled words of encouragement to each other, choked out as best they could between the gags.

So they lay there in their aloneness with their separate thoughts, sharing only the close touch of each other's bodies and the hard feel of the floor of the truck. Most of all they cursed their country, the rich, the landowners, the military. They cursed them for the lives they lived and vowed that they would have done what they did, even knowing what would happen. They vowed to continue the fight with renewed vigor and strength should they escape.

And then their minds went back to their families again and to the mundane, every day details of their daily existence, the all-so-important little things. They relived all the treasured small details that made up their lives, the joys, the pains, the suffering that had brought them to this end. Their thoughts weren't of deep philosophical significance, not of revolution, not of the big questions of the existentialist. They were simple thoughts of life, of surviving, of someday maybe having some land of their own, of someday not having to struggle so and fight against such odds. The only fight they desired was the struggles with nature as they sought to produce crops from her soil. They had no desires for power or wealth, just a life for themselves and their families.

And as they thought about their families and their lives and all they had been denied, some grew bitter and held their bodies stiff in anger in preparation for whatever may come, some felt tears forming and their body softened and lay limp along the floor, forming with the floor and moving easily with each bounce. They longed to sleep for a while and be healed by the body's natural healing power, but none could sleep, so they lay there with their thoughts, staring at the hard red metallic floor.

"I better get some more gas," Ivan remarked to Maria and Ruth. He pulled into a ranch near the village of Limones to buy or borrow some.

"I'm sorry, Padre. I have no gasoline that I can give you," the owner told Ivan then stood and watched as he drove off the ranch before heading back into his house to alert the army patrol.

"Ivan Betancourt just left my ranch in a blue truck with two women."

"Thank you for the information. We'll take care of him." The patrol officer informed Lieutenant Benjamin Plata and his men who had been waiting for such a call.

Fifteen minutes after leaving the ranch Ivan and the two women were intercepted and taken to Los Horcones.

The peasants paused briefly in their train of thoughts as the truck once again pulled to a halt. They listened to the indistinct voices of several men talking and as the voices diminished and yet the truck remained stationery, they thought that maybe this time they had reached their destination. Whatever was in store for them now, couldn't possibly be worse than the torture of that ride.

The voices came back and approached the back of the truck and they were ordered to get up. They were assisted in their movements by the two soldiers who had ridden in the back with them and now picked them up and shoved them onto their feet. It had been hard to lift their bound bodies.

Michael felt the bruises and the aches all along his body from the beating that morning and the rough ride. As he was shoved to the ground, his feet buckled under him letting him fall face forward onto the ground. Another soldier kicked and shoved him back to his feet as the remaining two campesinos on the truck were also shoved to the ground but managed to keep their stumbling balance.

Michael's head was swimming and he could hardly feel that he had legs, but he must have had, for somehow he managed to follow the other prisoners to where Ivan and the two women were waiting for them.

One of the peasants looked up and saw Ivan and attempted to speak his name through the gag. He was instantly hit in the back of his head with a rifle butt and fell to his knees.

"Get back on your feet." The man managed to lift his body back on top of his legs.

"What are you going to do with these men? What are they doing here?" Ivan and the women had not been gagged and Ivan's fierce Colombian spirit refused to be quiet.

"Silence, priest, or do you want us to do to your pretty women what we did to this man?" The soldiers standing guard over Ivan jabbed him in the back with his rifle.

Ivan lurched forward from the blow. He glared angrily at the solder but remained silent. Only the threat to Ruth and Maria Elena could make him hold his tongue as Major Chinchilla and Jose Manuel Zelaya sauntered toward the group.

"Okay, take the gags off these men and let's see what they prefer, castration or death." Major Chinchilla motioned to two of his men to remove the gags. "Let's see what kind of men they are."

He went down the line asking each one individually his preference. Each chose death over castration. As Chinchilla approached Fr. Cypher, he too prepared to choose death and began to open his mouth to state his choice. Chinchilla stopped him.

"Wait, priest, for you there is no choice." The five men were led off to their deaths, fear showing through their eyes as they bid silent goodbyes to Ivan. Only the two priests and two women were left. Ruth and Maria Elena held on to each other and looked over at Ivan for support, not knowing what to do or what would happen next.

The women were shoved aside as Zelaya stepped forward and ordered that the men be stripped and beaten. He flicked the whip he was carrying a few times before applying it to the two men, taking great pleasure in lashing the priests. He particularly relished each stroke brought to bear against Ivan's back because of the strong grudge he held against the priest. He wouldn't let anyone else but him be the deliverer of this justice upon the condemned man.

His lust for vengeance only partially appeased, he then ordered that Fr. Cypher be castrated and shot. Michael withstood the defilement of his body and thanked God for the merciful shot. The women cried out at the sound and began to sob.

"Shut those women up," Zelaya demanded. Ruth hushed Maria Elena, comforting her with an embrace then defiantly accepting the back hand of one of the soldiers. She continued to support Maria Elena who sobbed quietly while Ruth watched what ensued, firmly standing her ground.

Zelaya walked up to Ivan.

"Your argument is with me, Zelaya, not those women. They have done nothing. Let them go," Ivan insisted.

"Perhaps I should make you watch them die before I kill you?" Zelaya suggested.

"If you have any faith at all, if you fear God, let them go," Ivan continued to make his case. "They are innocent."

Zelaya walked over to the women and raised his whip, about to strike.

"Wait, I'll be quiet," Ivan said, seeing that any efforts on his part to help the women only made their situation worse.

Michael had been mercifully shot. Not so Ivan. He had provoked too much hatred and this hatred desired to feast itself on the bit by bit destruction of his body. Zelaya walked back over to Ivan.

"Take your last look at the man you condemned. I now condemn you to death." With these words he took a large iron spike and gouged out Ivan's eyes. The two women huddled together, Maria Elena hiding her face in her hands, thinking only of Bernardo and wishing she had never left her country of Colombia. Ruth watched with a horrid fascination that wouldn't let her tear her eyes off of this man despite her anguish.

Zelaya then stepped back and gave the orders one by one, first to pull out each of Ivan's fingernails, then his teeth and tongue, then they slashed off his testicles, his hands and legs. Ivan passed out from the pain before the final blows ended his life. His dying thoughts were for his mother, waiting for him in Juticalpa, unaware of the fate of her son.

This done, Zelaya then retreated with Chinchilla into the ranch house for a victory drink before breakfast, giving the order to their men to take care of the remains of the bodies.

"You know where," Chinchilla ordered.

Zelaya looked over at the two women, holding each other for support.

"Get rid of them," he ordered and went back to his house.

The bodies of the two priests were thrown into a nearby well, along with the bodies of the five peasants. The two young women were thrown alive into the well on top of the corpses then Lieutenant Plata tossed in two sticks of dynamite to seal the hole which was later covered with earth. Betancour's truck was driven back to the main road, doused with gasoline and set on fire.

-8-

Besides the round up and expulsion of the priests and nuns of the Diocese of Olancho, much church property had been destroyed or confiscated by the ranchers and the military. The government had been forced to investigate the deaths after a silent march of protest by the students at the University of Honduras, the outcry of the peasants who had loved Ivan, and the embarrassing questions being asked by the U.S. and Colombian governments. The mutilated bodies of the priests and the others were found and examined, speaking their own tales.

Gonzalo Galves, a local businessman, confessed to his part in the events of the night and implicated Major Jose Enrique Chinchilla, Jose Manuel Zelaya, and three others. He then died under mysterious circumstances. Further investigation showed that Chinchilla and Zelaya had not acted on their own but were only following the campaign planned against the church in Olancho two months in advance by the cattle ranchers of the region with the support of the National Federation of Cattlemen and the business community. These people had been well-trained in such methods of cold warfare and subtle attacks, especially those members of the military who had been trained in the U.S. as the "Pentagon's Proteges." Their instruction included courses on using and containing rumors and instruction on the use of propaganda.

One such course included information on the use of rumors. "The rumor (definition) specific or generalized proposition, to make someone believe in a thing without there being any concrete proof. Its diffusion is generally verbal, by word of mouth. Characteristics: its source is not obvious; it doesn't require a normal system of communication, thus its importance increases with the scarcity of such means; this technique is more important the lower the literacy rate; by divulging it in a situation of friendly confidence it tends to seem more trustworthy; objective verification is generally difficult. Basic Law of the Rumor: $PR = I \times A$. PR = Power of the Rumor; I = Importance of the theme it refers to; A= Ambiguity present, lack of concrete facts that would allow its negation or verification. Motivation: 1. Fear – tends to impart reality to the fearful anticipation of people who are 'ready for the worst,' demoralizes; 2. Hope – for people with a sense of frustration motivated by unfulfilled desire, the rumor relieves the tension of wishing, objective – complacency; 3. Hatred – provide an escape by giving them someone to blame, objective – create internal disunity. Reason for dissemination of rumors: in an atmosphere of crisis or tension caused by an emergency situation, the individual is predisposed to listen to and repeat whatever he hears, whether it be a rumor or true information."

There had been rumors aplenty during those months. The students had learned their lessons well.

Chinchilla and Zelaya were awaiting trial pending further investigations. Zelaya was now in residence in the Central Penitentiary in Tegucigalpa, in a three-room brick building he had been allowed to build for himself complete with wife, television, refrigerator and telephone. Zelaya was confident that he would soon be given his freedom and removed from the excommunication he was under because of his role in the murder. After all, as he said, "I am a Catholic and the godfather of over six hundred children. I am completely innocent."

The four of them set up headquarters in Juticalpa were Paul had been named interim pastor. Although Paul's speaking ability was still limited, he could understand most everything that was said to him and spent his days going out with the others, visiting different communities and learning as much as he could about the general situation of the people. Upon their arrival, they relieved a native Honduran priest who had been arrested, then let out and allowed back into Juticalpa, so he could get a break from handling such a large responsibility single-handedly.

They continued to have two Masses a day in the capitol and also staged a three month memorial Mass in memory of the martyrs of Olancho, as those who had been killed were being called. There had been some danger at the time but not enough to prevent the memorial from happening. The place had been packed. Peasants from all over Olancho had arrived by foot or horse in order to remember their beloved Padre Ivan and the others who had died.

They had only spent a month in Juticalpa but that was long enough for Paul to get into a conflict with a leading politician when he refused to allow him to be a godfather without first attending instructions. His lawyer came out and stated that it had all been planned and that the bishop had given the man permission to be godfather without attending the classes. Paul used his authority as interim pastor to say, "No," at which the politician was very upset, especially since being a godfather was considered an honor and he wanted to add on a few more godchildren to his chain of a couple hundred.

"Why should someone who has been a godfather so many times have to attend classes? Do you know who you are talking to?" he insisted.

"Do you know who you are talking to?" Paul responded. The man ended up attending the classes, same as everyone else.

They sent back reports to the rest of their group who were still in Tegucigalpa, explaining what they saw and asking that no one else come out until they were able to get back with their report in person. Kevin and Joe didn't see why they needed to wait. To their thinking if it had been that dangerous Paul and the rest would have returned right away. They were anxious to get back and see for themselves what was happening so they returned.

At the end of the month Paul and the others returned to the capital. Then started a week of meetings before going back into the diocese. It was decided that it would be best if Miguel Berel left Catacamas. He wasn't happy with the decision but because of the safety factor, agreed with the wisdom of leaving. He, too, had been marked for death by the landed and military and had been fortunate to escape.

Enrique Moulin along with Miguel would work in Juticalpa with the native Honduran priest who had spent the summer there. Throughout his stay at San Francisco and then more so that past summer, Enrique Moulin had had quite an influence on Paul. A committed, domineering man of over two hundred pounds, he knew how to throw his weight around. He was a French diocesan priest who had originally been working in El Salvador until he managed to get his name on the hit list there and was told by the church not to come back. He had dark hair and glasses, his glasses heightening the very clear vision he had as to what he felt he should be doing. Paul liked his commitment and only wished he had as clear a vision.

Paul and another French priest, Jean LeClerq, would be going to Catacamas and Joan and a French nun and Priest would be going to Culmi, just a short distance from Catacamas. It was late October before Paul and Jean made it to Catacamas. Jean was fussing about something and wasn't ready to leave, so Paul waited for him. He had made a quick journey to San Francisco and back to get his things. He didn't take time to say a word to anybody. He didn't like goodbyes, never liked them. He just wanted to get in and out, leave the place behind and go on to the next place. He had mixed feelings about the place, but basically it had been a good eight months. Still he was ready to leave and did not allow himself to dwell on the past.

Paul flew into Juticalpa one day while waiting for Jean, but then heard there was a threat of something or another - there was always the threat of something - so he flew out that same day, back to Tegucigalpa. He whiled away the rest of his time watching the World Series on TV.

Finally they left for Catacamas. Joan had already been in Culmi for several weeks by then and was quickly starting to feel at home with the Pechu Indians of the area. Once again she rode by burro into the mountains, visiting campesinos. On her days off she enjoyed the acres of natural forest in the area. The beauty provided a relief to her spirit, troubled by poverty and violence.

Living with Fr. Jean, Paul felt far from at home. Jean never seemed able to make up his mind what he wanted to do so he kept trying to do everything, leaving little for Paul to do. First he decided that Paul should work in the city and he would work in the campo because he felt he was better suited for this work. A week later he decided he was wrong and maybe he should work in the city, too, not giving up his work in the communities of the campo. Paul could work in the barrios. But no, that wasn't right either as Jean decided maybe he should work in the barrios as well. Paul bought the groceries each week, something Jean was not inclined to do.

Then Jean kept talking about leaving, but maybe not.

Because Paul still lacked proficiency in Spanish, he was hesitant to push the issue. He wasn't sure what to do. Even when he challenged Jean, he had difficulty getting his point across because of the language barrier so he just let it go.

Finally Paul ended up with a small town down the road from Catacamas, Santa Maria de Real, a few communities in Catacamas, and the old parish car - a huge blue Nissan patrol van.

Everywhere was evidence of Ivan's work. His presence, strong while he had been alive, was even stronger now as a martyr. It was said that when Ivan first came to Catacamas the church emptied as those with money left after feeling the sting of Ivan's words. But then the local people, the peasant farmers, had started to fill the pews to overflowing, inspired by his words as well as Ivan's presence among them.

Quickly the priests and religious in the diocese were turning Ivan's death and the deaths of the others into a rallying point for the campesinos, attempting to bring good out of a basic evil as only God can. The cattle ranchers found that dealing with Ivan dead, could prove to be harder than dealing with him alive. Paul found that out, too. Along with inheriting the parish car, he inherited the ghost of Ivan. He was not Ivan, didn't try to be Ivan, and, in his mind, the people didn't forgive him for this.

Ivan had been very much into the popular religiosity of the area which meant processions, everywhere, for every occasion. Paul had seen this popular religiosity in San Francisco. There, trying to give the people what they wanted he had agreed to hold the traditional procession on Good Friday, got a quarter of the way through it, then called the whole thing off and forbade everyone from using the parish basketball court the next day as punishment. The people had been walking wherever they please, helter-skelter, talking, yelling to each other, drinking, exchanging kisses and in general having a good time. It had been a far cry from the somber procession that was warranted on Good Friday. Paul stopped the procession but not the good time as the party continued on after he was gone. In his eyes it had lost all the meaning it originally was to have. Most of the popular religiosity, as he saw it, was an excuse to have a good time and had nothing to do with religion, nothing to do with social justice.

Ivan's strength as a person had been such that he had been able to put meaning into the popular religiosity and started with the old traditions of the people in his evangelizing. He had kept the processions with statues and even organized a pilgrimage to Culmi, a local sanctuary and holy place that people would travel for miles to visit. Dulce Nombre de Jesus - Sweet Name of Jesus Shrine. The people walked the several-day pilgrimage, singing and praying. It had worked, on the strength of Ivan's personality.

Ivan also had a lot of different groups meeting, the beginnings of base communities. Each barrio had a Bible study group meeting weekly along with day long gatherings each month. And then there was his marriage enrichment course which would run every night for a week. In a society where the definition of male and female roles was so strictly structured, it was hard for Paul to imagine how any real communication between the sexes could be accomplished without first attempting to equalize the relationships more, and yet this was precisely what Ivan had been doing, helping couples who often didn't know the first thing about sharing time together, to learn that there was more to marriage than working all day and having kids.

Ivan both encouraged and demanded a lot of participation from the people. He had a committee of people helping him with the marriage course and one hundred and fifty couples who had attended and were now helping teach the course. His Masses were always filled with singing, enthusiasm and participation on the part of the people, including a dialogue homily where he would go down among the people and talk to them directly, inviting their response. At every opportunity he would leave the altar to walk among his people. He spent as much time away from the altar and with the people as possible. He did everything himself, no cook, no secretary. He walked everywhere he went. Paul didn't know how he did it.

Always he encouraged the people to action, to work to better their lives and the lives of others in their community. As he wrote in one letter, which became treasured after his death, "No queden dormidos muévanse por alguna cosa importante en la vida .no basta criticar .hay que hacer algo… no nos cansamos de buscar algún modo de progresar. pienso que es muy trite quedarse uno estancado como ciertas aguas podridas a un lado del camino. Hay que progresar, no importa cuantos años tenemos, siempre se puede ir un poco mas adelante. Nunca hemos terminado." "We can't stay asleep, waiting to be moved by something important in life. It is not enough to criticize, we have to do something too ... We can't stop searching for ways to progress. I think that it's very silly to wait, stagnant, like rotten water next to the road. There has to be progress. It's not important how old we are, one can always go a little further. We have never finished."

Even after Ivan's death and the period when there had been no priests in the area, the groups that Ivan had started continued to meet. The only problem was that, at times it seemed the people had been more committed to Ivan than to the gospel he had been trying to teach, making it doubly hard for Paul and Jean. Initially they had continued Ivan's work, except for the marriage preparation classes as neither of them had the training or the interest to continue them. And since Jean tended to do everything, Paul found himself once again with a lot of time on his hands to think about what to do, how best to do it, trying to understand these people better, where they were coming from, what made them what they were. So far he felt he only had a surface knowledge of who they were both because of cultural and language differences. He wondered if he would ever come to understand them, much less be accepted by them.

Their history had been a long one of exploitation, same as all the other Latin American countries. Columbus first set foot on the land of Honduras in 1502. At that time there had only been a few indigenous tribes of Indians in the country, a society without classes, without private property or possessions. There had been certain Indians marked as slaves with clay obtained from a fruit growing wild in the country. However, it was not slavery as commonly known in European culture, but rather a form of penal punishment of prisoners from enemy tribes that were forced into labor for the good of the whole tribe, not belonging to individuals. The idea of private property had been completely foreign to them, and unnecessary.

With the descent of the Spanish conquistadors in 1522, slavery became a way of life along with private ownership of land. Then, in order to protect Spanish ownership of this land and possessions, laws, courts, soldiers were established, protecting the rights of the privileged few. Prisons were established for those who disobeyed the laws.

This has been the history of the people since that time. All the land and wealth in the country remained in the hands of the few who controlled the laws and the military. Winning independence from Spain made no difference. It was a matter of changing hands. The government went from the hands of the Spanish to Honduran-born Spaniards. Essentially nothing had been changed as far as the social system or economy. It had seemed by far the better alternative to weakened Spain to hand over the country rather than wait for a revolution from the people. Honduras achieved its independence bloodlessly, while basing its structure on a form of legalized bloodletting. And then came the Americans.

The Honduran Indians did not take kindly to being made slaves and had fought and struggled against the conquistadors. Had the church not intervened, chances are the Indians would have been completely wiped out as had happened in the Dominican Republic and at Haiti. Paul found it hard to see the fierce, fighting blood of their ancestors in the simple peasants of today. Their simplicity and lack of regard for personal possessions remained as they shared readily whatever they had. This was especially so the further into the mountains you went, the farther away from modern society and its influence.

And he, too, the farther he was from the country of his birth, was starting to see differently. Not that he had ever been a raving patriot, believing "My country, love it or leave it". He had considered himself quite open-minded in his thinking, willing to question and criticize his government when this was warranted. He had taken a firm stand against the Vietnam War in his youth. It was other firmly planted beliefs coming from his childhood growing up in America that he was seeing differently. Beliefs that everyone could pull themselves up by their boot straps if they only had the guts and the know-how. Beliefs that looked down on anybody who didn't "make it" in America, land of opportunity, because it was his or her own fault. Nobody else's. If you had to step on someone to be a success, that was their problem, not yours. In the land of opportunity the other person had as much opportunity to step on you as you had to step on them. If they didn't, that was their problem. And if you made it and your neighbor didn't, that was their problem, too. You weren't your brother or sister's keeper. America - land where the individual reigned supreme, land of equal opportunity to exploit.

"You, American," a local landowner had stated to Paul. "You think you are so much better than we are. Land of the free, home of the brave. Land where anyone can make it if they just worked hard enough. I spit on your country," he spat on the ground as he said this.

"Who do you think you exploited in order to have what you have? Where are your Indians? Who do you have to exploit in order to continue your lifestyle? Ask yourself that. You are no better than us, amigo," he said and walked away. Paul had not known how to respond. It was only with Joan that he was able to discuss such matters. Joan knew where he was coming from because it was where she was coming from too.

"America, land of opportunity," he stated.

"If you say so."

"I don't say so. The American dream sure looks different from down here. America is supposed to be the land where a person isn't judged by their family connections but by their personal accomplishments. We created a good life, a middle class, but who did we have to step on to get there? What about the Native Americans? Everyone can have the good life, the American dream, a house in the suburbs, two cars in your garage, TV, stereos, vacations at Disney World, if they work hard enough, we say. Who do we have to continue holding down to maintain our society? How much of our wealth depends on exploiting third world countries?"

"It is a land of opportunity for some," Joan asserted.

"Is it? If the only way for us to maintain our way of life is through exploiting people in third world countries, then maybe it's not a dream but a nightmare. How can I look in the eyes of the poor in this country knowing all I had growing up when they had nothing, knowing how our country's policies have helped to create and sustain the poverty here, knowing our government, the CIA, is behind much of the violence? It was so much easier when I didn't know anything."

"It's not your fault where you were born, any more than it's my fault where I was born or where these people were born. It's a world of sin, original sin. All of us are born into it. It's up to us, once we recognize the sinful nature of our world, to do something about it."

"Easier said than done."

"I didn't say it was easy. Some people go through their whole lives never once opening their eyes beyond their own narrow point of view. Thank God you can see what you do. It's a blessing."

It was a blessing, but one Paul hadn't asked for. Paul knew all too well who was being exploited so that he might have the middle class life-style he had enjoyed while growing up. He saw them every day. The realization was none too pleasant for he had to admit that he was culpable, even though not knowing. How can a person be responsible for a sin he or she knew nothing about? Social sin. Original sin. You are born into this world for better, for worse, and as you are part of this world and the world is one of sin, you are a part of that sin. It sounded simple in the theology books.

It wasn't simple in reality as you looked into the eyes of the people who had been exploited so that you could have your lifestyle. It wasn't simple and it wasn't nice. It hurt.

Paul didn't want to feel the injustice, feel the hurt, didn't want to feel at all. His head ached as he tried to hold back the feelings. He felt like the blind man in the gospel who saw people as walking trees as he slowly gained his sight. He couldn't see clearly, try though he did. He wanted a clearer vision, to understand what he was to do. He wanted to be like Enrique in his vision. But there were still too many things in his way, ways of seeing the world, years of indoctrination from his past, his family, the culture he grew up in. He, too, needed liberation.

"Lord, grant that I might see," he cried out in prayer. These people needed liberation. Maybe they could liberate each other, he thought to himself.

-9-

Part of understanding this culture and its people was spending time visiting them in their homes. Paul considered this a very important part of his ministry. Whenever he was in someone's home, whatever they offered him to eat, he ate and liked, whether he actually did or not. He had a pretty strong stomach and a good appetite so he rarely had any problems.

All day long, Christmas Eve, it was one big celebration, going from house to house to house. In every house he was offered naca tamales, made especially for that occasion so he couldn't turn them down. Naca tamales were made out of ground up pig guts, rolled in masa -corn. Later, he finally managed to escape back home for a while before heading back to Santa Maria de Real at eleven p.m. to prepare for midnight Mass.

The people slowly began drifting in, late. He wasn't being as strict here about starting on time, and besides, this was a special occasion. As the church began to fill up with people chattering among themselves and keeping up the party atmosphere from the day, Paul had an attack of cramps in his lower half. The attack passed, so he continued to get everything all set for the Mass. He looked out at the crowd sitting in the half-lit church holding candles and decided it was time to get started when he was hit by another cramp and realized he better find a bathroom right away.

"Maria!" he called to the young woman who had been helping him get ready.

"Si, Padre."

"¡Necessito un servicio, rapido!"

"Si, Padre, vamanos," Maria took one look at Paul, grabbed her shawl, and together they rushed down the altar and out the side door of the church.

"¿Que paso? Where is the padre going?"

"I don't know."

"What's going on?"

"Do you think we missed the Mass?"

The chatter which had died down as Paul and Maria walked out on the altar, slowly picked up as people turned to their neighbor and asked if they knew what was going on, then strained their necks to see if they could see anything.

"Maybe he is going to process in from the back of the church," one ventured and all heads turned to the back in silent expectation. Several men near the front got up and looked out the door. All they could see was the priest and this young woman running down the street then turning into a house. They stood and chatted with each other, made some speculation and started laughing. Soon everyone in the church was back into their party mood, laughing and chattering and drifting out of the church.

Paul quickly sidestepped the house to find the outhouse in back. It was dark outside and pitch inside the outhouse. Paul had to grope carefully around to find the hole in the ground before he fell in it. He also didn't care to place his hand in anything that may have missed the hole. Finding the hole he planted his feet, pulled down his pants, and squatted, despite the cramps that made him want to fall over. All he had to do was maintain himself in a squatting position over the hole and Mother Nature did the rest, relieving him in small streams.

As the cramps eased and he seemed to be approaching the end, he became aware of the stench. He wasn't sure which stench was worse, that coming out of the hole, or that coming from his behind. It really didn't matter. They were both enough to make you want to add even more to the stench by vomiting.

With the last squirt, he thought maybe now he could leave and get back to the church so he slowly raised himself up, paused a moment to steady himself and make sure he wasn't going to have to squat again, pulled his pants up and prepared to face the world again.

Maria had waited discretely in front of the house but was becoming concerned. She was about to go back and check, when Paul came around the corner.

"Muchas gracias, Maria," Paul said with a sheepish grin. They headed back to church.

By that time there was no one left but a few stragglers.

"Where is everybody?" Paul asked.

"Someone said you had left with a girl, so when you didn't come back they left."

Paul went ahead with the Mass with the few that were left.

Around the middle of January, Paul was approached by a small delegation of people from Santa Maria de Real to say a Mass each day of their feria - fiesta - the first week of February.

"Please, Padre, every year we have the feria and every year we have Masses."

"No, not this year. This is a year of mourning for the martyrs. How can you have a feria when you are in mourning?" It had been decided at one of those many meetings in Tegucigalpa before returning to Olancho that they would observe a year of mourning for the martyrs.

"But, Padre, every year we have the feria. It is a tradition. We have booths. We have games. We have a parade. We even have a queen. All the girls will be disappointed because they won't have the chance to be the queen. And the children will be disappointed. You don't want to disappoint the children?"

"I'm sorry, but no. I won't go against something agreed upon by the diocese and that I agree with. I'll be there the Sunday following for a Mass and baptisms, but that's all."

"Okay, Padre, adios," the delegation went away very disappointed. Paul wasn't about to back down. He knew about this feria. At one time it had had religious significance but now it was just another profit-making venture. They had added games and booths and, like so much of the popular religiosity, the feria had lost all religious meaning.

The people who stood to make a profit from the feria weren't happy at all. They began to talk among themselves about ways to get even. They finally decided that they would show that priest and changed the lock on the church.

"Some padre he'll be without a church," they commented.

The old lock was removed and replaced with a new one.

When Paul drove up in his big car, there already was a crowd gathering outside the church.

"What's going on?" Paul asked as he walked up to the large wooden door. He saw the lock, turned around and stated that there would be no Mass that day, but he would perform the baptisms since many families had come from a long way for them.

The men who had changed the lock weren't pleased with this turn of events. They proceeded to unlock the door. The people who had come for the Mass and the baptisms weren't pleased either. Both groups started yelling and chaos ensued.

Paul walked up to the altar area as the people poured in behind him, still yelling at each other and him. The people who had been upset about not having the feria went about provoking others to yell louder. Paul attempted to shout everybody down but his voice was not up to the job. He climbed on top of the altar table to quiet everybody down. Everyone was too busy yelling at their neighbor and shaking their fists to bother with this priest dancing on top of the altar. Paul gave up trying to quiet them down, stood looking at the chaos, then threw up his hands, climbed down and fought his way out of the church and into his car with people bumping against him, screaming at him and threatening to shoot him the whole way.

Paul got in his car, started the motor and pulled out of the crowd of people. He drove back to the rectory in Catacamas, took a shower, fixed himself something to eat, poured some coffee and sat down with some reading until Jean came home and asked him how his day had been.

"Fine," he said calmly, "except I lost a church today."

Paul continued his regular meetings with the people of Santa Maria de Real, having outdoor Masses and other ceremonies and meeting in small groups in homes. The loss of the church building seemed no great disaster. The ministry of the church went on. However it gave Jean another chance to change his mind and try to make Paul full-time housekeeper while he took over the church at Santa Maria de Real.

"But then," Jean said, "maybe I'll be leaving soon to go to the capital to study."

Despite Paul's problems with popular religiosity and all the processions, he and Jean decided to go ahead with the traditional ceremonies for Holy Week, starting with a procession on Palm Sunday, a procession of men on Holy Thursday, and a procession with a casket on Good Friday as they re-enacted a holy burial, stopping every couple of blocks for prayers. It hadn't been as chaotic as in San Francisco, undoubtedly helped by Jean's command of the language and Paul's increased ability to communicate. Still Paul had little patience with these traditions that to him appeared to be little more than an excuse for a party.

Since this was their first year in Catacamas, they went ahead with the tradition, not wanting to make a lot of sudden changes, however the processions weren't that well attended. Perhaps without Ivan they were not as meaningful to most of the people. Perhaps they truly were looking for something more than an excuse for a party, Paul mused. Ivan had somehow made the processions meaningful. They did get some response, more than a small response, but not the attendance Ivan used to get. The people who did show up were the ones who were locked into traditions. They went through the rites simply because they were a tradition.

But perhaps the people wanted more than a theology that told them to accept their lot in life and hope for better in heaven, Paul wondered, trying to assess what to do. He was trying to meet the people where they were in order to lead them to something else.

He kept informed about what was happening elsewhere in Latin and Central America, the atrocities in Guatemala, El Salvador, Argentina. He was particularly intrigued by what was happening in Nicaragua. Somoza's regime still retained power but there was a growing insurgency movement there. Guerilla warfare had grown as the people sought a new way of life, revolution. Honduras had been through so many revolutions and military coups in its existence. Was what was happening in Nicaragua more of the same or was it different? Was this truly a revolt of the common person? He heard that there were even priests involved in the effort, not necessarily carrying guns but supporting the guerillas. He wondered about this. How could they align themselves with the guerillas? Yet he didn't know what he would do if the same situation occurred in Honduras.

Gandhi himself had said that some conflicts could not be resolved non-violently. Better to stand up for yourself, speak out against injustice, than to be a doormat. Gandhi's revolution had been against the British Empire, a civilized nation of reason. Would it have worked against a mad man like Hitler? Or a man with no conscience like Somoza?

More questions. Everything led to more questions, "The more I learn, the more I realize how little I know," he said to Joan. "The more I learn the more questions I have."

"I do know one thing. The bishops at Medellin got it right when they said the Church needs to stand with the poor. Where would Jesus be if not with the poor and downtrodden?" Joan responded.

"That I can agree with," Paul agreed.

Some people didn't want to stir up trouble or work for change. There were many different charismatic groups springing up in the area. Paul wondered where they got their funding. They managed to get extensive AV equipment for slide-shows and films and musical instruments for their weekly prayer meetings where they preached joy, joy, joy. The Honduran government was supporting them, he suspected. After all, it kept the people happy. The American government funded them indirectly, providing foreign aid with strings attached that designated money for such groups. Many of the leaders of the groups came from the U.S. as missionaries. And they received support from the rich.

The groups were largely made up of non-Catholics. The Catholic Church was still a power to be reckoned with from the long years of Spanish and Papal influence. The numbers of the charismatic groups never grew to a significant amount, just enough to be annoying.

"You Americans?" one missionary approached them.

"That obvious," Paul mumbled to Joan. He had hoped to avoid any association with members of the group.

"Yes, we are," Joan answered, extending her hand while giving Paul a look.

"I just wanted to introduce myself," he accepted Joan's outstretched hand then reached for Paul's. "I'm Reverend Walters. We are going to be holding services tonight in case you are interested. Would love to have you join us."

Paul wanted to say no, come up with some excuse, or even better, tell him the truth about what he thought about their services. Joan stopped him.

"Thank you. We'll see if we are available. What time?"

"Seven. Look forward to seeing you both," he responded then left.

"Now why did you do that?" Paul complained.

"It won't hurt us to be sociable, maybe see what they are doing. You never know where you might find an ally."

"Waste of a perfectly good night, if you ask me," Paul responded. He begrudgingly went with Joan that night, arriving slightly after seven and slipping into the back of the tent where he hoped no one would see him.

Paul wanted to leave as soon as they got there. The gospel of joy, joy, joy, was not for him. He was uncomfortable around all of the release of emotions and the speaking in tongues. Paul wasn't into the gospel of joy. He was into the gospel of justice. He saw little reason for joy in the hard lot of the campesinos. He thought they, too, were looking for more than hope for a better life in the next world. That was what he wanted to give them, something real that touched their lives for better now. Joan, for her part, checked out the AV equipment.

"Wouldn't it be great to have that for our workshops? Maybe we could borrow them," she whispered to Paul, nudging him and pointing with her head.

"Why not? Probably funded by our government. We might as well put it to good use." Joan poked him and shook her head to keep him quiet.

"Can we go now?" he asked once the last song ended. Too late. Reverend Walters spotted them in the back and stopped them before they could leave.

"Father, sister, good to see you." Paul sullenly waited his opportunity to leave while Joan made arrangements to borrow their projector and screen.

They had the traditional Easter fire on Holy Saturday night with the blessing of the water. On Easter day a group of people went down to the river for some fun. The river was a focal point for activities as many hot days were made endurable by a dip in the cooling waters. Young people spent their holidays splashing in the shallow waters which came about chest high on a grown man in the deepest section.

The whole day was spent by the river as the children played and watched the young men of the town form a human tower three stories high. Then the children imitated them, building a tower of their own. Paul had joined in the fun, relaxing from his duties and thoroughly enjoying himself. It had all been a lot of fun, even if it meant getting a little sunburnt, but a little sunburnt certainly didn't explain the way he felt the next day. It had to be more than the sun.

Paul was scheduled to go to a three day meeting in Tegucigalpa, along with all of the other priests and religious in the area. He decided to fly in because he didn't think he would be able to manage all the bouncing around that was part of any drive in Honduras. He managed to make it through the meetings till he could get to a doctor for a blood test. Diagnosis—hepatitis, he had joined the ranks of those statistics affected by the lack of a sanitary water supply. That meant several months of bed rest. What better place to get bed rest and tender loving care but home in the states, under the watchful eye of his mother.

He returned to Catacamas just long enough to pack a few things then headed to the states.

GOING INTO ACTION

III

Se puede decir que a estas altenas del proceso nos
encontramos ya en plena tarea de concientizacion… Hemos
descubierto que esa situacion y este mundo material no puedan ser
dominados si no es en estrecho relacion de accion y coordinacion
con otros hombres. (Proaño)*

One can say that at this advanced stage of the process we now
find ourselves fully in the task of conscientization… We have
discovered that this situation and this material world can't be
dominated if it isn't in the narrow relation of action and
coordination with others.

-11-

Her head was throbbing. Was it any wonder? Up at four a.m.?
What was she thinking? Of course she would end up with a
debilitating headache, forcing her to leave work at ten a.m., just
two hours after she had arrived. Cancel all her appointments, she
had told her secretary as she headed out the door. Now if only she
can make it home safely, half blind as she was with pain. She
managed. Somehow she managed. She always managed, did what
needed to be done at the time, and so she did today.
　　She pulled down the shades, closed the curtains and collapsed
on the coach. Slowly the tears came out. She couldn't let them out
in all their power. It would have hurt her head too much, such
wracking sobs. And yet holding them back was hurting her as well.

78

She remembered those trips up into the mountains of Olancho that summer of 76, the year after the massacre. Paul had been gone, dealing with a bout of hepatitis. It was his turn this time. It seemed hepatitis was just part of any mission experience. Try though you might to avoid it, no matter how careful you are to wash your hands, avoid drinking untreated water, the virus manages to slip by and into your digestive system. She had had it earlier that year forcing her to spend February to May back at the motherhouse in Michigan. How she had hated it. How she had longed to be back. It wasn't so bad at first when she had been too sick to be bored. Once she started feeling better the days had dragged on. She spent time with family, which helped. Still she wanted desperately to be back in Honduras. Paul had sent a few cryptic letters relating events in his life. She could fill in details herself. It just made her want to be back all the more. How she missed the mountains and the people.

When she did get back, she moved from Culmi to Catacamas. There wasn't enough work to warrant so many religious in Culmi. The shrine was watched over by a priest and some local sisters. There was also a French priest and sisters. They could handle the work load adequately. The need in Catacamas was much greater. Joan moved into a house in Catacamas with another sister from her order.

Joan quickly went back to doing what she did best, visiting in the mountain region. As she had gotten more comfortable doing this, she would stay for weeks at a time, sleeping wherever there was room for her. How she had loved these people and the mountains, loved the long rugged rides for hours on mule, bumping along, peering over the edge of steep cliffs as the mule walked as close to the edge as possible. She had loved it despite what it was doing to her back, a recurring problem to this day. And the people loved her.

She ate what they ate, slept where they slept, struggled to learn the Indian dialects prevalent in the mountains, and shared their lives. The campesinos considered it a great honor to share their meager food and simple homes with her, and she in turn considered it a great honor to be received into their home, share in their lives and struggles. She drank coffee with them, shared their meals of beans and rice. She always got the best of what they had and was fed before anyone else. At first she had found this custom very hard to accept. It was hard for her to accept that she was always given the best, no matter how little that was, but slowly she learned to accept it as part of the culture and redoubled her efforts to raise awareness among these people, teaching those who had taught her so much, helping them realize they had rights.

Still it was a struggle, both within her, and within so many of the other people working with the campesinos. She struggled to know whether what she was doing was right, the struggle with trying to teach them and yet not push them in any direction too much but leave them free to decide for themselves. That was the struggle. Theirs wasn't a ministry of insurrection, inciting revolution, as claimed by some. Theirs was a ministry of teaching the people that they had rights, teaching them to work together and support each other as communities. A ministry of teaching gospel values which said that all people were created equal in God's eyes, that all men and women are truly brothers and sisters and called to help each other.

They struggled to not put their own personal bias in their teaching, yet it was impossible to avoid this completely. They struggled to raise the awareness of the people to a level where they could make their own decisions without being overly influenced by others, society, or their culture. It was a theology of change, radical change and in this sense, revolutionary, but it wasn't a theology of guns or force. It was theology of liberation that set people free, as Jesus set people free. It was a theology to free them to be themselves, to be all that God meant them to be. Theirs was not to tell the people where to go, but to free them to hear that inner voice of God and decide for themselves where to go and then to support them in their decisions, wherever that may lead them.

It had been a constant struggle, both dealing with these people's cultural hang-ups from years of oppression and having their rights denied, and dealing with their own cultural hang-ups as Americans.

Joan's journeys in the mountains often led her to strange bedfellows as she slept with grandmothers, aunts, little children, sometimes crowded five or six to a bed, and sometimes she'd wake to find animals slumbering on top of the covers or sheltering underneath, mostly domestic animals such as chickens or pigs. She also shared her bed with the little slimy creatures of the land, snakes, scorpions, lizards, iguanas, and of course the ever present cockroaches, fleas and mosquitos. She had run into some larger wild animals at different points in her travels such as pumas and jaguars, but those were very few and usually from a distance, causing little reason for fear.

She also had seen a few large boa constrictors hanging from trees, or lying bloated in the sun, but for the most part the dangers were no worse than backpacking through the Rockies in the U.S. and the run-ins with these animals were few and far between. And then there were also the many colored birds that flowered the land in the higher reaches, the toucans, macaws, quetzals, all with their splendid plumage and colorful beaks. And the monkeys screeching in the forest at night and performing during the day, especially the little spider monkeys.

Joan loved this country. Each journey in the mountains made her more committed and more determined in her efforts for the people. So she pushed and pushed her body and traveled far and wide throughout the country, her hair caught back in a ponytail at the nape of her neck and her head held high, always wearing a smile for the campesinos. She had loved the fresh air and the sound of children welcoming her as she arrived on her burro. She had made sure to bring back lots of small gifts and candies from the states to be given to the children. She had also brought back simple medical supplies to keep her first aid kit well stocked with bandages, gauze, rubbing alcohol. She was getting quite adept at simple first aid, at times being referred to as doctor sister. She had used some of her time at home to get further training in CPR, splints and other basic first aid skills, knowing the need for them.

-12-

For Paul, the four months "recuperating" had been much better for him than Joan's. First he went to stay with his sister and her husband in South Carolina where the doctor told him he could do whatever he felt like doing. He was up the next day and out on the tennis courts. Then he went back home to Michigan where this doctor told him to immediately get in bed and stay there. So he stayed there for three weeks while his mother was in her glory, having her son home to take care of. Within a month he was pretty much up to par but still taking it easy and enjoying his vacation.

The Honduran people remained with him, though. He was so happy to be back, happy to see Joan waiting for him at the airport.

"It's so good to see you," he said as he gave her a warm welcoming embrace.

"Good to see you, too. So how was your time in America?"

"You know," he said, and yes, she did know.

"It was so strange to be back in the U.S. after almost two years here," he said.

"Yes, reverse culture shock. It is worse than the original culture shock of going to Honduras in the first place. I expected that. No one had forewarned me how hard it would be to go back."

Paul's three weeks in bed had delayed and softened the shock but it was still real. He had to keep reminding himself that this was the USA, events started on time here, everybody had a car and ate at McDonalds and ate meat two, sometimes three times a day, instead of beans.

"So weird to hear everybody speaking English and to not have roosters waking you up in the morning in the city and driving down a street without having a chicken, goat or pig suddenly pop out in front of your car. And all the white people."

Joan laughed, "Pretty scary, huh?"

"You said it," Paul agreed then continued. "It was the little things that got to me the most, times when I'd feel completely disoriented, having electricity at the flick of a switch, watching TV, drinking clean, cold running water straight from the tap. Simple little things that used to give me pleasure before now meant nothing. Going to my home church, the fourth of July parade and picnic, steak on a grill, I know that once I had enjoyed these, but now . . . Do you know what I mean?"

"Same thing for me. I think the term is expatriate. We no longer belong in our own country."

Yes, but do we belong here, he thought to himself. He had become accustomed to something else. He stayed in the states just long enough to become re-accustomed to these little niceties of life, but now he was back.

"Oh, and the fat. Since when have Americans become so fat? I don't remember it being that way." Only the rich in Honduras could afford to be fat, he thought.

"And teeth. Americans have full sets of teeth. And waste, if something breaks or tears or someone didn't care to eat something, it was thrown out." What Americans threw out in one day, Hondurans could have lived on for a year. Necessity is the mother of invention. Poverty brought out tremendous inventiveness as they created new ways to patch items to prolong their life. But he also had found he could live without all the gadgets Americans find so necessary. He could live without a toaster, electrical can opener, blender, juicer, sweeper, TV, stereo. Instead of listening to records you made your own music.

And somehow, even without all the conveniences to make life easier and free us in the states for more important things, it was the Honduran people who always had time to talk. They were never so busy rushing from one appointment to another, that they couldn't stop what they were doing to talk. Conversation was their chief means of entertainment. Conversation was becoming a lost art form in the U.S. Somehow in the American world of gadgets, making lives easier, there never is time for talk.

"Did you do the speaking circuit?" Paul asked.

"Some."

"I had to hold my tongue, watch what I said." Paul had been critical before going to Honduras, but now . . . he had fuel for his fire. He found himself being asked to speak to various groups about his mission experiences. They had been hoping to hear tales of starving children being fed, stories of miracles and conversions and God working in the wilderness of this foreign country. Well, God was at work, but not how they had expected.

"How many of us Americans today realize what is actually going on in Latin American countries? All we hear is what the news media tells us, but what our newspapers tell us is completely different from what you hear once you are down there. The violence, torture, repression, violation of basic human rights. There are evils occurring in most Latin American countries today that are every bit as horrifying as those perpetrated on the Jews during Hitler's time. Are we going to sit back and pretend we don't see? Do you think that somehow that makes us less to blame? What will future generations say about our generation? 'How could the Germans have allowed such things to happen?' people ask. How can we sit here in our comfortable middle class environment and not see what we, as a people, are doing? First world countries have their middle class because of the exploitation of third world countries," was what he had wanted say, but didn't.

"How little they realize," Paul said.

"How little we had realized until our eyes had been opened," Joan reminded him.

"They don't realize the amount of U.S. involvement in the government and military of Latin American countries. That the U.S. government protects and supports dictators and oppressive regimes in order to maintain the life we have, protecting American interests," he added. In 1903 and again in 1923, the United States Marines had been sent into Honduras to protect American lives and property and to aid in "settling internal disturbances." How concerned had they been about the lives of Americans in Honduras during the massacre of 1975, he wondered. How concerned had the ambassador been about getting his sister out safely and sending word to their family?

How little they knew. Trickle-down theory: Help those on top and somehow it would trickle down to improve the lives of those on the bottom. There is only so much wealth in the world and so, the rich get richer and the poor get poorer. Paul wanted to say that to them, all the people at home, but he wasn't able to do it without a lot of anger and emotion pouring out which just wasn't his style. He tried to be controlled. He didn't even allow himself to yell inside so the words remained unspoken, even in his head.

"They won't know unless someone tells them," Joan reminded him.

"I tried, as much as I could. I tried to be diplomatic, but that's not exactly my strong suit." He had spoken to the Knights of Columbus and different church groups, showing his slides, pointing out differences in lifestyle between there and here, hinting, hoping they would get the point, draw their own conclusions, refraining from saying what he wanted to say.

"Anyway, it's great to be back. It's so good to talk to someone who understands. I know my family and my friends in the states mean well, but they just don't get it." Joan knew exactly what he was talking about.

"So, time to get back to the business of changing the world," he said with a grin. It had been such a slow process of becoming accustomed to the culture, slow and frustrating. Now he was ready to really get to work, be effective, put into action some of the ideas and views that had been growing in his head. He was ready to take on this land and its people once again.

It had been also good to get back to the big old house that was the rectory. Like all other rectories and convents in the area, it had been built years ago for the friars at a time when the church in Latin America had been building beautiful edifices to itself and for the people who worked for her.

It had been a large Franciscan house, built in the traditional square Spanish style as all the houses built at that time were. There was the traditional lush garden with a never-ending bloom of flowers all year round, right in the middle of the house. Orchids, begonias, roses all blooming forth like big bushes and spreading to the edges of the veranda and the small tiled walkway running through the garden. Tropical plants and cacti filled in among the flowers. On the east side was a thigh-high wall with pink begonias blossoming on top, separating the garden from the covered hall in front of the four individual doors that belonged to the bedrooms.

It was a delight to get up each morning, step out the door to such beauty without leaving your home. Rain or shine, you were protected under the pillars and ceiling so that you could sit along the hallway of pink and white square tiles and enjoy the sight of a tropical shower replenishing your garden while little lizards, constant guests of the house, ran about the wall and stared down at you, darting out a long forked tongue then scampering on. They were your constant companions in the house, preferring the cool walls to the hot sun and since they ate cockroaches, other constant companions, they were welcome additions to the house, almost like a house cat, but better because there were no messy litter boxes or cans of smelly cat food.

On the west-side was another hall, separated from the gardens by pillars and the change from the tiny white tiles to the large pink and white tiles indicating where the garden area left off and the hall began. The wall was opened by large arching windows that showed through to the large meeting area and the office which was the first part of the house you saw as you entered.

On the south side was the church, on the north the kitchen and dining area which led to the back garage. And out in back was the big backyard enclosed by a large high wall, which at one time had served as a center for many activities planned by the friars. Banana trees, grapefruit trees, orange trees, avocados, mangos, papayas, just about any kind of fruit tree imaginable was growing in the backyard, providing fresh fruit to the priests and their guests and a welcome diversion for Paul last year as he would walk out each morning and gather the ripe fruit as part of his "grocery detail."

Even with the cracks in the plaster and chipped paint, it was a beautiful house, although a chore to keep clean. Paul appreciated the fact that there was no sign above the door prohibiting entrance "a particulares". While Ivan had been in Canada, some Spanish priests had been there and put up the sign, which Ivan immediately took back down when he came back. One of the Spanish priests then left with the young woman who had been cooking for them. The other stayed till Christmas before escaping to a more comfortable lifestyle, finding life with Ivan not all that easy.

Paul could never understand how Ivan had managed without a housekeeper or secretary to answer the constantly knocking door. Paul had hired a young woman from the town to do the housekeeping and cooking. She was there, broom in hand, sweeping the kitchen when he returned.

"Buenos dias, Lucia."

"Buenos dias, Padre," she responded, smiling in welcome. She walked with a limp due to an attack of polio as a child and was quiet and shy around most people, especially these priests. She had been very happy to get the job and very grateful to Paul. She went about her work quietly with a smile on her face and her hair pulled back in a neat bun and rarely spoke unless spoken to first. Paul was slowly working on getting her to speak up more but so far hadn't been too successful.

He dropped his bags in his room then went back to join Joan and meet the new priest, his new co-worker and house-mate. Joan had filled him in on the new priest during the drive. Jean had finally decided to leave and was now in the capital doing research. Clemente was a young newly ordained Honduran priest and into the good life, from all Paul had heard. Suffice it to say that in the short time that Clemente had been the only priest at Catacamas, the rich were beginning to come back to church.

Clemente was a young, good-looking Latin American, more into "soccer" than work, as far as Paul could tell. He figured it was going to be a long year, sighed, and prepared to deal with Clemente and the rich.

-13-

Paul went back to his work of visiting families and base community development, while Clemente visited the rich. Clemente smashed Paul's blue Nissan, which did very little to raise him in Paul's estimation. Paul dragged him from meeting to meeting, taking him to different communities and trying to make him toe the line. He never directly said Clemente had to do what he was doing, just went about his work with a few verbal suggestions that he help out and more non-verbal suggestions. Each was free to do what they wanted. Paul would explain why he did what he did with the hidden assumption that–what was the use anyway, it wouldn't do any good.

Paul also journeyed by mule into the mountains, visiting different villages and staying with the people, following Joan's example. However the padre always slept alone, except for the few night visitors that crawled into his hammock or bed. For the most part though, the mountains were Joan's domain and he and Clemente remained in the city and the regions close by.

No excuse for a fiesta was ever missed by the people, so this year his birthday saw another party complete with the piñata which was a traditional part of any birthday. Just as Paul was preparing to be blindfolded and have a go at hitting the piñata, in walked Rosa and some others from San Francisco, carrying the little burro he had gotten for his birthday two years ago and had left in his room there. And following them all, was Kevin. Paul was pleased to see him again, despite differences from the past. He was especially touched by the appearance of Rosa and the burro he had left behind. He didn't know who had organized the trip but he was glad they had come. Later he had a chance to spend some time with Kevin.

"How goes it?" he asked.

"Good, very good. We broke ground on the orphanage just a week ago. It should be finished next spring. How goes it with you?"

"Good. I'm working on a different type of building project, building small communities, building a movement."

"You are not going to do anything crazy like those priests in Nicaragua, are you?"

Paul just smiled, "So good of you to come. Who organized this?"

"I did. I wanted to see how you were doing."

"I'm doing fine. Thank you. Maybe I'll get a chance to see your orphanage when it's done. Keep in touch," Paul said, knowing full well that chances were neither of them would. Not out of animosity, just out of lack of time and the fact that they were moving in different directions from each other.

The festive birthday party was followed by another party, not quite so festive, Bishop D'Antonio's farewell party. Since the massacre, Nick had been staying in Tegucigalpa rather than Juticalpa. He had been told not to go back to Juticalpa since his name was still on the list of those slated for death. He had been told by Rome's delegate to Honduras to leave the country. Reluctantly he finally gave in, feeling his hands tied in such a way to make him no longer effective here. All the workers in the diocese had been sorry to see him go.

Paul gave him a strong embrazo. "Thank you for bringing me here," he said.

"It was God who brought you here. I was just the humble instrument," Nick replied.

In his place Celestino Pennisi was named as Apostolic Administrator by the superiors of the Franciscan order in Central America, a man with no pastoral experience whom the apostolic delegate figured would be easy to manipulate. The quiet, mild-mannered man with thick glasses and greying, thinning hair, constantly went about in his long brown Franciscan robes, giving him a monkish air. He treated his priest well but was out of touch with what was really happening in his diocese and hence–was easily used.

In the short time that Paul had been back, he had noticed a change in Clemente. A marked change over October and November so that by early December Clemente had experienced a complete turn-around in regards to his ministry and what he thought he should do.

"Maybe," Paul wondered, "maybe it had sunk in, some of what I've been telling Clemente, some of the experiences he's been having . . . nah, it couldn't be," he wondered out loud to Joan then decided himself that it wasn't possible. This was something he hadn't seen coming. Paul hadn't seen the small indications of Clemente's thinking as his eyes took in the scenes and saw what Paul was all about until slowly, hidden inside him the change in Clemente had taken shape.

"Don't sell yourself short," Joan had told, "or Clemente either," she added. Despite her original misgivings about the priest, she, too, had been seeing signs of change. He had only recently been ordained and knew nothing more than his seminary training. Left on his own that summer he had maintained the lifestyle he had been accustomed to without thinking he should be doing anything different. Then this strange American priest came. He hadn't seemed to like Clemente that much yet he showed him a new vision of ministry and a way to help the situation of the poor–the situation Clemente had grown up with and had grown accustomed to seeing. It hadn't occurred to him that it could be different but having responded to a genuine call to ministry he followed that call and quickly altered his tack when shown an alternative way of dealing with what had been a part of his life for so long.

At this time the French sisters and priest from Culmi began to come more and more often into Catacamas to work since there was not enough work for them in Culmi. Eventually they moved to Catacamas. Armand moved in with Paul and Clemente, the sisters moved into the house with Joan.

With Clemente's change, he and Paul moved into a full program of base community formation, helped by the newly arrived French priest and religious. 1977 got off to a good start. All six were working well together, with their different areas of responsibility. They all shared the same vision of ministry and commitment to the poor. This commitment which was still in formation in Clemente was becoming stronger daily in Paul

Along with their regular program of catechism, they had a youth group with a solid core group of ten to twelve people which was meeting on a regular basis at the parish center and at the rectory. They also had meetings occurring regularly within different communities. These community meetings, once started and going strong, usually continued without a lot of assistance from Paul or the others, except an occasional visit to keep in touch.

They organized many workshops for the people dealing with the problems of their day-to-day existence in Honduras, using many posters and other visual aids and encouraging the campesinos in turn to make their own posters using pictures cut from magazines and telling in their own words the reality of their situation: illiteracy, alcoholism, malnutrition, lack of medical care, prostitution, machismo, and exploitation in all circumstances, every area of life. They tried to get down to the root cause of the problems, the lack of land, power and wealth residing mainly in the hands of a small elite and not in the hands of the majority of the people, and they tried to teach them there was power in the people, that they could do something to better their lives if they organized and worked together cooperatively. They tried to show the advantages of working together to better their lot and the lot of their brothers and sisters, rather than working alone.

They devised games to introduce the simple campesions to the complicated affair of money management, credit and big world business and banking so that when these people went into the city with their produce, they wouldn't be quite so easy to cheat and would be aware of their rights. Often times the workings of banks and big business and the capitalist system of trying to get ahead seemed very hard for them to comprehend. They would see through the complicated maneuvers of the capitalists and so clearly show in their lack of comprehension a wisdom far greater than any of the rich, multi-national business people.

"But why would I want to gain money and other things if my neighbor doesn't gain too?" they would ask. They could hardly understand the mentality that sought individual good over the good of the community. They had to learn about this mentality so they could deal with it when they found it, yet go on to something better, maintaining the sense of community and responsibility for neighbor. This is not to say that as the campesinos were exposed to capitalism and various members began to acquire more possessions than the others, these members never became every bit as possessive and power hungry on a small scale as the people in power higher up. At times they ran into problems in communities where one person would try to seize leadership and power, becoming a small dictator to the detriment of the whole, but then their job was not to confront this person themselves but to work with the other members of the community to show them that they could speak against this person if they disagreed and challenge him or her themselves.

It was slow, hard work. Often it seemed they were getting nowhere fast.

"You know," Paul commented to Joan, "maybe we should start a building project, maybe a school or a clinic. At least then we would have something concrete to show for all of our work."

"You aren't serious, are you? I know the results aren't always forthcoming or evident, but there are rewards. Like when Pablo spoke up for himself when they tried to short him on his crop payments."

"Yeah," Paul remembered that, how excited Pablo had been. He had come to tell him about it afterwards.

"Padre, I saw them trying to tip the scale in their favor to cheat me and my family. They thought I was just a stupid campesino, but thanks to you I knew better. I saw what they were doing and started to take my crops elsewhere. Then they removed their hands from the scale and I got a fair price. I remembered how you told us about this, to watch out for it."

Paul had been pleased. "But that was just one time," he said.

"One time of many. You never know how many others you may have had an impact on. But I know what you are talking about. It is hard. Sometimes I wonder if I couldn't be doing more somewhere else, in a different ministry. I try to help, try to educate, without running their lives, telling them what to do. I try to help them run their own lives. It would be so much easier to do a more traditional ministry."

"But not more fulfilling," Paul said, their roles reversing. "And it is evangelization. It's pre-evangelization, laying the groundwork to lead them to the gospel. Feed them bread first, then feed them God's word, help them see that God is relevant to their life."

They encouraged the campesinos to voice their opinions in written form, working in solidarity with other campesinos not only in Honduras but in other countries of Latin America. They wrote to communities in neighboring El Salvador, expressing their support for their efforts to persevere in the face of persecution.

Skits were very popular among the campesinos. They loved the chance to get up and play act as with a few hats and pieces of material they improvised their scenes or read from scripts prepared beforehand. Most often the stories revolved around campesinos who somehow bested the powers that be, whether that be a shopkeeper, a rich landowner or a police officer. The skits touched close to home as many of them could relate similar experiences that had actually happened without the campesinos coming out on top. The skits gave them to chance to win for a change, if only in make believe. They gave the actors and the audience a chance to express many feelings about their situation which otherwise may have remained unspoken, not realized until brought out through the medium of the play.

Paul and Joan stood at the back watching as the campesinos laughed at their own acting. They smiled at each other in a silent congratulation for their efforts.

14

Carried on by the momentum of what seemed to be their success with small communities, Paul, Armand and Clemente decided to dispense with all the traditional processions of Holy Week, except for Palm Sunday. They had cut out many of the other traditions of the people in their move to concentrate on small community formation. They also decided to publish a monthly newsletter as a means of communication among different communities.

The team began to use the radio as a way to reach more people. They had a live Mass on radio every Sunday and their own rip-and-tear radio program daily where they would point out local injustices and ask how these could be equated with the gospel message of Jesus. Clemente was becoming quite good at speaking on the radio and was soon lambasting the local rich stronger than any of the others. It was good to have a native Honduran doing this so they couldn't be accused of being outsiders coming to stir up trouble.

Just as they began to work well together as a team and seemed to be making progress, an on-going conflict with the local leaders and the official Church leaders began to grow. Relations between them and those leaders were progressively strained.

The Apostolic Administrator, Celestino, had sent his hatchet man, a man named Blas Torchino, to Juticalpa to take up residence in the bishop's house rather than coming himself. Miguel Berel had since moved to Campamento to work. Enrique Moulin and Francisco continued to work in Juticalpa. Francisco was officially the pastor, however Blas Torchino took over, deciding that the chapel and rectory needed to be done over, all with Franciscan money, money unavailable to support the work of the priests.

"The money you are using to redo the church could have supported over a hundred families for a year," Enrique had challenged him.

"And a beautiful church will provide spiritual support for over one hundred years," he had responded.

Blas quickly made friends with the rich sector of the town and set about undermining and undoing the work that had been done in the diocese, especially taking on the team at Catacamas, both from the pulpit and the radio.

In May Clemente decided to leave to attend the marriage preparation course in Canada that Ivan had attended several years ago, with the idea of starting the program up again, but mainly realizing that there was so much he still didn't know about this ministry. Paul hated to see him go. Despite the bad beginning, they had grown close from working together. Paul had to admit that he had misjudged him at first.

Relations with the local police were none too good either as they received many threats. The police moved into a building across the street from the rectory in order to be able to keep an eye on their comings and goings.

On June 8, 1977, Paul looked out the window of the rectory, through the rain, at a truck parked across the street in front of the police station with a man sitting in back. Something seemed to be wrong with the man based on the slouched way he was sitting and the pained expression on his face.

"Joan, look at this," Paul called to Joan to join him at the window. She set down her coffee cup at the table where they had been chatting and stared out the window.

"I'm going to check it out," he told her. "You stay here." Joan followed him out. As he got closer to the vehicle, it became apparent that the man had been shot. Blood was caked on the spot in his shoulder where the bullet was lodged, trapping the shirt into the wound as part of the scab. Paul knew of a reporter who usually ate around this time at a restaurant a couple blocks away. He sent one of the gathering crowd to get him. Paul figured this was something the reporter would be interested in.

"What are you doing? He needs to see a doctor, not a reporter," Joan tried to push by to help.

"Stay back," Paul told her. "El doctor, pronto," he directed another young man. "There, they are going to get a doctor," he told Joan. "Go get some blankets to wrap around him." Joan went back to the rectory. While she was inside the reporter showed up and began to question the man about who had shot him. It was then that the police came out.

"What do you think you are doing?"

"I'm questioning this man."

"You have no right to interfere. This is police business."

"I have a right to ask questions."

"This is official police business. You have no right to interfere in it. You better move along."

"I have a right to be here. You can't just order me around."

"I order you to move on."

"The people have the right to know what's going on. I have the right to ask questions. Why hasn't this man been taken to the hospital?"

"Move on."

Paul moved to the back of the crowd, looking for Joan who arrived with blankets. By then the conversation had gotten more heated as the reporter refused to leave. It was no longer possible to get through.

"We better go," Paul told Joan, keeping her from trying to force her way through. "The doctor's been alerted. There's nothing more we can do. Besides I have to get ready for seven o'clock Mass." Reluctantly Joan agreed to leave. They had both learned it was better to not get involved in police matters if they wanted to be able to continue to serve in the country.

The next day, over the radio, the reporter went on the air and related the whole incident, violently attacking the police and the lack of justice in the town. He ended his broadcast with the statement, "Thanks be to God we have Padre Paul Anderson in our town who really cares about the people."

Later that day Paul and Joan were driving along in the parish car (complete with a new paint job after Clemente's crash that past October) on their way to a baptism when a car full of people pulled up alongside of them and motioned to him to stop. Paul pulled over and they stopped behind him.

"What's going on?" Joan questioned as she turned around and looked out the window. A man got out of the car and came running after them with a gun.

"Paul, he's got a gun, get out of here," Joan screamed and turned around as Paul gunned the car, went crashing through a ditch on the side of the road, pressed the gas to the floor and took off down the road, trying not to think too much about the three gun shots he heard behind. He didn't know where to go, just knew he had to keep going so he kept heading down the road ahead of the car, glancing first at the car trailing behind and then at the broken gas gauge in his car, hoping he wouldn't run out of gas.

Finally they made it to the next town. He pulled in behind the local rectory and he and Joan ran for the back door - locked.

"We've got to climb over the wall," he said, helping Joan over the wall and following after her. He just made it to the top when the man who had shot at him showed up with seven soldiers.

The man began screaming drunkenly at him while the soldiers trained their rifles at him and motioned for him to get down.

"You almost ran me over," the man screamed, "I'm from DIN, the secret police. You better come quietly with me."

With the guns trained on him, Paul climbed down and began to walk down the street. Joan tried to see what was happening then sought out an open door so she could call for help.

"What's going on here?" The lieutenant of the local police station stopped them in their procession. He knew Paul and asked him what had happened at which point the man from DIN responded.

"He tried to run me down. We're taking him in for questioning."

"I've never seen this man before in my life, and I certainly didn't try to run him down," Paul replied.

The lieutenant told the others to be on their way then turned to talk to Paul.

"Don't worry about that guy. He's crazy. Never mind about the whole thing. Just come in tomorrow to make a report."

Paul thanked the lieutenant and went back to the rectory. He was about to open the front door when Joan opened it.

"Thank God you're all right," she said and hugged him. "What happened? I called the police. They didn't believe me," Joan rattled on. Paul pushed her back inside the rectory, walked in and was just about to fix himself a drink when someone came to the door. "Who's that? Don't let them in," Joan said as Paul walked up to the door and asked who it was.

"Police, we've come to get your report," Paul heard from behind the door. He let the officer in.

Paul had hardly had a chance to let the numbness wear off before he had to go back to Catacamas for Mass. Joan offered to drive. He readily gave her the keys. Mentally he realized what had happened, but the feelings hadn't caught up with him yet. He managed to get through the Mass in a state of nervous shock before going home and collapsing.

The next day at the radio station for their daily broadcast, Paul ran into the lieutenant of the Catacamas police station who was on none too good terms with Paul. Paul questioned him about the incident and didn't get a straight answer. He never found out whether this had just been a personal, one man vendetta against him, or whether it had been planned.

Later that day Armand suggested that they go to a movie to help distract Paul. By this time Paul was falling apart. He kept seeing men with rifles trained at him everywhere he went, hiding around every corner. He lasted for fifteen minutes in the darkened theater then couldn't stand all that he was imagining he saw in the dark and headed back for home. For some reason, there were extra police out on the street that night. That didn't help any.

He walked into the house then was stopped by the sound of stamping feet.

"My God, they are waiting for me. There's someone in the house," Paul said to himself, ran out the house and back to the theater where he pulled Armand out. "There's someone in the house."

They went to the back door of the house and could see a light on inside. Then they went down to the night school and asked a teacher to go to the house, knock on the door and see who answered.

The teacher came back after a while.

"It was only Hermana Joan," he told them. They heaved a sigh of relief, apologized to the teacher then went back to the house to join Joan. Joan had come to see how Paul was doing. She had been upset as well and had not wanted to stay at home alone until the other sisters came back from a church meeting in a neighboring village.

15

The news of their near escape hit the papers immediately, going nation-wide and finally reaching the United States. Paul hadn't planned on telling his parents about the incident. Instead they were informed by the newspaper. Joan escaped mention. She was just a nameless sister in the article, which suited her fine.

Paul's parents watched daily for any news about Honduras and were surprised to see their son's name in an obscure article in the Detroit Free Press. "American Priest shot at in Honduras." They got in touch with their congressman, who got in touch with the ambassador, who got in touch with the Honduran government and a decree came out to the effect that "there was to be no more shooting of priests," especially not with American guns.

That June 25 they had memorial Masses for the martyrs of two years ago. In the morning there was a Mass in Juticalpa and in the afternoon they rode back to Catacamas for another Mass. Both Masses were well attended.

In July, Paul was visited once again by a delegation from Santa Maria de Real, only it was a different delegation from the one a year and a half ago that later took over the church.

"Please, Padre, we have the church back. Will you come back and say a Mass for us?"

Paul and the delegation got in his car and rode to Santa Maria de Real. This time, as Paul pulled up in front of the church, the doors were wide open and singing could be heard coming from inside. People came up to the car and welcomed him. They all wanted their chance to tell him what had happened.

"We went to the mayor and city council," yelled someone in the crowd. The speaker stepped forward and continued. "All of us. We went together and said 'We want our church back.' We said, 'It is a sin in the eyes of the blessed Virgin and all the saints that her church should be kept locked for so long with no one allowed to visit.' And the mayor, he said, 'Okay.' He said whatever we want to do was okay with him. So we marched from the town hall, singing and dancing, and broke the lock and we've been inside ever since then."

Paul was almost carried through by the proud, happy crowd of singing people.

Over the summer, the team at Catacamas and other members of the diocese were becoming increasingly aware of the church's displeasure with them and their work, and of the leadership's desire to get rid of them. Word had already gotten back to them that Celestino was actively looking for more priests . . . to replace those he already had, they wondered?

It also began to become evident that relations among team members at Catacamas were deteriorating into a cultural split between France and America with Paul and Joan on one side, Armand, Louise and Michelle on the other side. The work continued but disagreements grew and personality conflicts developed. Somewhere along the line, the work in the town, Paul's main area, was not progressing as it had been. In fact, he seemed to be losing ground. All that he and Clemente had started so enthusiastically last winter, was no longer catching on. They were missing the people. The monthly newsletters were still relatively effective and well received, especially in the outlying communities, but in town, problems were developing. These problems though had to be put aside because of greater problems with the church.

Since he had been named administrator, Celestino had only been to visit Catacamas once, and his main concern had been for when they wanted to have Confirmation. It was the only question he had asked.

As the situation got increasingly worse, they began to prepare for whatever Celestino might plan on doing. The priests and religious in the diocese met together every four to six weeks. In October they began meeting regularly with lay people also so they would be informed about what was happening and ready for "it" whenever it happened. They tried writing to Celestino, asking him for a meeting with them to clarify his position on what was happening in the diocese but received no response.

What they feared "it" would be was the forced deportation of Enrique Moulin from the country. Their strategy: In the event that any movement in that direction occurred they would send out a code message over the radio to mobilize the people and would meet the next morning at Catacamas.

On Monday, December 19, Enrique received a letter from Celestino stating that he had been suspended based on his past actions and could no longer function as a priest until the suspension was lifted. Immediately the country was mobilized. Local newspapers and radio stations were contacted. The news spread throughout the country creating a national scandal. On the Friday following the arrival of the notice, a commission representing the priest, religious and lay leaders of the diocese appeared before Celestino. They came back on Saturday with no results.

They had been meeting daily to resist Celestino's proclamation and had decided that unless something positive came out of the commission's visit, there would be no Eucharistic celebration anywhere in the valley this Christmas because they were not one with their bishop. Rather than the traditional celebration of Christmas Eve Mass, the people of Catacamas were to gather that night for a prayer service of grieving. Many of the lay leaders had been supportive of their cause, both writing letters to the Apostolic Administrator and giving up Christmas with their families in order to take documents to other groups of people.

On the morning of Christmas Eve, Paul received a letter from the bishop in his home diocese in Michigan, informing him that he (the bishop) had been asked to co-operate in forcing Paul out of the country. He stated he was not going to do it, but thought that Paul should be aware of what was happening.

It was a bleak day for Paul. He could see the hand of fate stepping in and forcibly removing him from this country. He thought that this would be his last Christmas here. After so much investment of time and energy just to get to the point where he was beginning to see what he needed to do and how to move forward in his ministry, to be cut off from these people, from his ministry? What use had been his long years in the seminary preparing for ministry overseas? What use his three years in Honduras, learning the culture and language? What was worst of all was the affront to him as a priest by the Church, the Church he had given his life to in service, the Church he had believed in despite the corruption, the clericalism. Yet another blow from the institutional Church and the powers that be. At that moment he felt as powerless to fight back as the campesinos felt before their oppressors.

Still he was part of this institutional Church, whether he liked it or not, for better, for worse. He pulled out the folder with remembrances from his seminary years and looked through them. He paused at the copy of the service from his ordination. "You are a priest forever, in the order of Melchizedek," he read. The words from Scripture came back to haunt him. This betrayal by the church he loved was like discovering that the woman you had married four years ago, not only wasn't the woman you thought you had married, but that communication had broken to such an extent that divorce was inevitable. Yet the words from Scripture seemed to be telling him divorce wasn't an option. Once a priest, always a priest. He wondered if the damage could ever be repaired.

Joan found him sitting at the kitchen table that morning, a bottle of Scotch next to his coffee.

"A little early to start celebrating, isn't it? Even for Christmas Eve." He handed her the letter he had received.

"They are after me, too. I'm the next one to be forced out." Joan stood as she read the letter then placed it down and leaned across the table to confront him.

"So what are you going to do? Are you just going to sit back and do nothing? I think you want out. You were just waiting for an excuse to go back to the states and your comfortable life there."

"You really don't know me if that's what you think."

"Then show me. Come up with a plan. You always have a plan."

"Maybe it is just as well. Things aren't going well. Every time I think we are making some headway, something happens and I'm back where I started, or even worse off. Maybe I'm not meant to be here, not cut out for it," Paul mumbled.

"You are right about one thing. I don't know you," Joan said and left.

Paul wondered what was wrong with her but gave it little further thought as he mused on his situation.

The rectory had become more of a home to her than the house she shared with the other sisters. They were nice and all, but they didn't seem to have a lot in common. They went about their different ministries, shared the events of the day. It was pleasant but nothing beyond the surface. Despite her misgivings about Paul at first, they had been able to develop a friendship. They shared ideas, beliefs. They didn't talk about feelings, but that was okay. They were swept up in something greater than themselves and that was fun, exciting, scary at times, but there was no need to talk of feelings except for maybe about how they related to their work. They were living the gospel, putting their lives on the line for their faith. What could be more romantic than that? She didn't need hearts and flowers, just some good Honduran coffee and conversation.

Theirs was a friendship, nothing more. She knew that, only now and then, she wished for something more even though it was forbidden, even though she knew what a terrible mistake it would be. They were friends. That was enough. She cared about him as a friend.

Paul had no such thoughts, or at least if he did, he never gave any indication of it. It was all work for him. His door was open to everyone. He enjoyed having guests drop by and enjoyed Joan's company. Yet if she were gone he would hardly notice, Joan thought with a sigh. Yes, he would notice the same as he would notice anyone, any of the long line of campesinos whom he had befriended, but not more than them. She wanted to be special to him, more than the others, but not more than that. Did that make sense, she asked herself? It hardly made sense to her.

She had gotten into the habit of dropping by any time during the days that she wasn't in the mountains for a light breakfast or noon meal. She knew she would always be welcome, and she liked that. The other priests were nice as well, especially Clemente. Armand was stand-offish, didn't talk to her much, but didn't seem to be too annoyed by her presence. Clemente was much more voluble than the other two priests, warmly hugging her when they met, chattering away. He treated her like one of his sisters. She felt very comfortable with him once she had gotten to know him, after those initial months and her negative first impression. She had been very sad to see him go when he had left to study. Still Paul was around. Somehow the give and take wasn't quite as easy with

Paul as it had been with Clemente. With Clemente gone and Armand withdrawing into his own little French world, she spent more time with Paul, when she wasn't in the hills.

She spent so much time moving around from one place to another; it felt good to have Paul's stability to come back to. The rectory felt like home. The home she shared with the other sisters was just where she slept at night, where she ate meals; the rectory was home, where she laughed and talked about work. Still, she wondered, how much did she really know Paul?

-16-

After Christmas everyone was back at work, meeting, reporting, sending and receiving letters. A representative from the Church of Mexico came to help mediate the crisis in the Honduran Church. On the following Wednesday, Enrique and about fifty other people went to meet with Celestino. Celestino both lifted the suspension and apologized. The next day he sent out a public statement supporting the work of his sisters, priests and lay people.

Everybody left after the meeting except Paul and Joan. Paul had an appointment to meet with the archbishop of Honduras. Joan stayed for support.

Paul entered the plush office of the archbishop, sat uncomfortably on the end of the chair across from him and proceeded to ask for an explanation about the letter he had received from Michigan.

The archbishop sat back behind his desk, leaned back in his chair, clasping and unclasping his hands on the desk in front of him. Finally he clasped his hands and leaned forward in his seat.

"I sent the letter at the request of the Apostolic Administrator of Olancho. I was only being supportive of Celestino Pennisi in his role as Administrator, going along with his recommendations and request. It was in no way an attack on my part of you or your ministry here, simply a supportive action for Celestino and his ministry. I also sent similar letters to the bishops of the home diocese of both Enrique Moulin and Armand Belin, as requested by Celestino. There had been no action on my part other than that."

103

Paul was dismissed after that, the archbishop having nothing further to do with him.

"How did it go?" Joan asked as he slid into the car. She slid over, giving him the keys, abdicating her place as driver.

"Well, at least I wasn't alone. He also sent letters about Enrique and Armand," Paul said as he turned the engine on and started driving. "Let's get out of here," he said as he took off for Catacamas.

Paul never saw Celestino after those rounds of talks. He left sometime around the end of March. A new Administrator was appointed in April. Rumor had it that Celestino had either suffered a heart attack or a nervous breakdown.

The tremendous response from the people to the crisis had been very rewarding and heartening. Maybe they were making headway after all, Paul had thought. But once the crisis was over, it was back to work as usual and now the difficulties that had been pushed aside during the crisis, became more and more apparent. The split between the Americans and the French became wider. It was natural that, due to cultural and language differences, Paul and Joan would relate to each other more easily and the French speaking team members would relate to each other. But, perhaps because they had already spent so much time together before moving to Catacamas and had an established relationship, the group seemed a closed community where the Americans were tolerated, but only tolerated, not accepted. Still the work continued.

This April, for Holy Week, Paul brought back the Holy Thursday procession of men, only this time they marched in silent protest, speaking only through the signs they carried denouncing evil and injustice as seen in their daily lives. April also brought the new Apostolic Administrator, a man who was also bishop of another diocese in Honduras, doubling the amount of land and people he was responsible for. He, in turn, sent his own hatchet man to replace Blas Torchino in Juticalpa. He sent two men to do the job. They quickly set out to make the other priests and religious in the diocese look bad with the rich, not that this took much effort. Their main purpose was to get information about the work of the priests, religious and lay people in this diocese. They went from one rich house to another gathering this information, finding many eager informants. These men, too, openly attacked the work of the team at Catacamas. Their victory that winter had been short lived.

Joan's back had been getting progressively worse from all of the long mule rides into the mountains. When the doctor told her she could not continue her work in the mountains and ordered her to take some time for bed rest, she reluctantly agreed to go home for a few weeks. Paul decided this might be a good time for him to take some vacation as well to get away from the stress from his living situation. He left the last week in May, spent three weeks of R&R, then came back to a situation that had gone from bad to worse.

While he was gone, Armand had taken over. He fired Lucia, the housekeeper Paul had hired that first year at Catacamas, and entirely changed how the money was being handled, taking it out of Paul's hands. Paul felt like he was back in that first year at Catacamas with Jean who would not let him do anything. But this time Paul could speak the language and knew more than that first year. He knew the town and wasn't about to allow himself to be booted out by the French.

On the twenty-fifth of June, once again they had a memorial Mass for the martyrs. The simple plain walls were decorated with wreaths of flowers. Each wreath had an inner circle of white flowers, a circle of red flowers and an outer circle of white. Plain crosses decorated with red and white ribbons represented each martyr. The crosses and wreaths were spread throughout the church below the colored Stations of the Cross and interspersed among the few statues and stained glass windows. Behind the altar, which had been covered with red and white flowers for the occasion, hung a banner with "25 de Junio de 1.975" written across the top. In the middle was a cross with the martyrs' names written alongside. Underneath the cross were written the words, "Los martires nunca mueren, viven en al corazon del pueblo," - the martyrs never die, they live in the heart of the people. Enrique Moulin joined Armand and Paul to concelebrate the Mass.

Before the Mass, Paul found himself in a screaming rage with Armand and the French sisters over the hosts for the Mass, such a little thing. He didn't know just where it came from or what exactly caused it. Just one more change while he had been gone, without consulting him. He had it. He blew his top, so unlike him. He was always under control, no matter how angry he got, he never let it out in this fashion, but he did. And then he had to go on and preach at the Mass that day. Somehow he managed.

Joan, back from her trip to the states, had overheard the shouting match and tried to ask him about it, but he dismissed her because the Mass was about to start. She watched sympathetically from the back of the crowded church.

After the blow up on June 25th, there was no communication at all. Everyone pretended it didn't happen. They all were in agreement as far as goals, vision and commitment to the people and their struggle. But when it came down to the details about how this was to be achieved, that was where problems arose. Paul was working with Louisa in the city. Whenever they reached a decision on any aspect of their ministry, Louisa would run to Armand and see what he thought. Then if Armand disagreed in the least, she would change her mind and they would be back to where they started from.

"Okay, so it's set."

"Armand thinks we should wait."

"But Armand isn't the one doing this, is he?"

"I think we should wait, like Armand says."

Armand seemed to enjoy playing the two of them against each other. He was abrupt and difficult to communicate with, yet there was no doubt about his commitment to the work and the people. He was reliable and followed through in the day-to-day tasks of the struggle, making it hard for Paul to find fault with him.

Joan wasn't able to be much help. Prior to this she had spent most of her time in the mountains. Now that she could no longer do this she needed a new ministry. Paul had thought she could work with him in the city, but Armand and the others vetoed that.

It had been a hard blow to her, being told she could no longer ride her burro into the mountains. She had been looking for something else to replace the feeling of fulfillment she had found in the hills, meaningful work. When this didn't surface at Catacamas, she knew it was time to move on, much as she hated to leave Paul. She had wanted him to hate her leaving even more than she did; had hoped that maybe, just maybe, he would go with her, or at least ask her to stay, let her know what she meant to him. But of course that wasn't about to happen. Paul stubbornly refused to consider moving.

"You have to do what you have to do, but I'm staying," he had told her so she packed her bags and moved on.

Paul tried to bury himself in his work. Once Joan left there was no one he could share his frustrations with. And then it seemed that somewhere along the way he had lost the people of Catacamas. They had never really gotten over their loss of Ivan, had yet to grieve sufficiently, he thought. Paul had neglected to help them through a grieving process. He hadn't tried to replace Ivan, but he hadn't been able to help the people move beyond Ivan, through their grief, to acceptance of him. All they could see was that he was not Ivan. Everywhere he looked, he saw ghosts of Ivan. And here he was, this priest who wasn't Ivan, who came in and made changes. He didn't love them the way Ivan had, they thought. They felt it - felt that Paul was motivated more by duty than love.

When a widow lost her only son, he visited the grieving mother at her home and performed the wake and funeral. He spoke about the widow of Nain, Jesus's concern for widows, and God's special care for widows and orphans in the Old Testament. It all sounded good and was scripturally accurate, but it lacked something.

"Padre Ivan, he would have embraced me, cried with me. When he preached, everyone would have been sobbing. This one, he is different, not like Padre Ivan," she commented.

"When I lost my job," another added, "Padre Ivan, he came over with food from his own table for my children. He helped me get another job so I could support my family. He was like my own brother, part of my family. This one, he visits but he is not family."

Paul didn't know what else he could do besides what he was already doing. He was stuck but saw no way out, no way of changing the situation. There was something inside him holding him back from giving himself fully to the people. Was it possible that he had no love to give at this time?

Paul kept going on coffee, cigarettes, and movies. He went about his work, gave the appearance that everything was fine, but inside himself it was dark, bitter, angry, alone. He wondered, maybe he shouldn't have come back from his vacation. He had been told by a "seer" while on vacation that he shouldn't go back to Honduras. His family had never been happy about him being there, and since the incident with the gun shot, not a letter came without them pleading that he get out of that hell-hole. He had come back out of a sense of duty. He had an obligation to these people, he thought.

"But what about your obligation to yourself, your family?" his sister had written. Her words were not convincing.

He released some of the anger he had built up inside in his preaching against the rich landowners and the government. He felt trapped with no way out. The more impossible the situation became, the more impossible it was for him to leave.

-17-

Still the work went on. In anticipation of the third bishops' conference in Pueblo, Mexico, ten years since the bishops' conference in Medellin, each of the small communities wrote letters to the bishops in support of their work with the poor. It gave him some sense of accomplishment to read what the people had written, knowing that he had had some small part in helping them to find their voice.

Catacamas, Olancho, Honduras
July 18, 1978
Bishops of the III Conference of Bishops
We, the undersigned, members of the communities that form the parish of Catacamas, direct ourselves to you. By means of this present, receive a greeting in the name of Christ, Liberator, and we proceed to communicate to you the following:

1. That the advances that the Latin American Church has taken in these ten years since the second meeting of Bishops in Medellin follows ahead as this: the creation of a Church more participative and at the service of the poor; the sprouting forth of base communities; the participation in the search for a more just society, proof of which are the countless number of martyrs that, following the example of Jesus, offered their lives as, for example, here in Olancho, those of Talanquera and Los Horcones.

2. That the Bishops in Puebla follow the example of Medellin denouncing the injustices of which the Latin American people are victim. In particular we speak of the bad distribution of the goods of the earth that God created for the service of all, lack of respect for the dignity of the people on the part of the authorities and the powerful; low salaries; unemployment; high cost of living; administrative corruption; the making of women into objects for business purposes; an education system far from reality that is lived today; large investments of money in the purchase of arms, instead of proportion it to the people for medicine, means of communication and technical assistance to the campesinos.

3. That you present before the assembly the voice of the oppressed, so that it can be a Gospel of liberation as it is said to us in Luke 4:18-19. This is the message that we should follow. For this we ask you, how many times have you visited the prisons, hospitals, the barrios of marginalized people, isolated communities in the mountains? As Pope Paul said, in order to know God, it is necessary to know people and it is in all these centers that one meets the oppressed.

For these we hope that at the moment of making decisions, it be the Holy Spirit who lives among her suffering and oppressed people, who illuminates you and you choose in favor of the poor. We will be with you and closely following the happenings of these meetings and we hope that they will be a benefit to our people.

The Community of Santa Maria de Real

Catacamas, Olancho, Honduras
August 6, 1978
Estimed Monseigneur,

Receive a greeting from this community desiring much success in your apostolic labors. Besides this greeting we manifest the following:

1. Monseigneur, we are conscious of the human, social promotion of liberation that we have in our people.

2. We, as campesinos that we are, most closely know the reality in which we live.

3. We are in accord with the documents of Medellin because of the fruit that they have given to our community.

4. We ask that the third analysis of the Conference of Bishops will be to the benefit of the campesinos that are now the majority.

5. It is of vital importance that you analyze the problems that we have; economic, social, political, cultural and religious education.

6. We hope that in this third Conference the changes will accelerate themselves in order that we not be a sleeping or passive Church. We desire a liberating Church in order to reach that which we desire.

7. We would like you to consider that in our people and communities, human rights are not respected, we are strongly exploited, we lack medicine, we don't have adequate food nourishment, the majority of us live in cardboard houses, the majority of us are illiterate. We would like to discover who has the guilt for all this injustice.

Without saying more, we politely take our leave.

The Community of Gloria de Pataste

Sept. 3, 1978

From Culmi

We, animators of communities, have analyzed the Latin American reality in light of the documents of Medellin and reflecting about the next meeting in Puebla, we hope for the following: That the conferences in Puebla analyze the economic, social and political situation of the Latin America, that every day oppresses the people by way of the powers that have robbed rights from people who are the image of God. That you take into account the problems of the campesinos.

We desire that you follow and amplify the Documents of Medellin.

From De Sosa, Moncho writes:
I want to say to the bishops who are going to meet in Puebla, that it will be very important that they deal with the situation of women, because this hasn't been taken into account. They have qualified it as a dead matter, knowing that God created man and woman with the same dignity, the same rights, and that we are capable and equal to men, to think, to work for a new world order.
Many think that we have been born only to make tortillas. I would like that they talk of our rights as the Christians that we are.

From Sabana Larga
Sept. 6, 1978
We hope that the advances that the Latin American Church has gained during these ten years continue forward:
The creation of a Church more participative and at the service of the poor, the surging forth of base communities.
The participation in the search for a more just society.
The martyrs of Olancho—Talanquera and Horcones—are a sign that the Church is Christ.
That the bishops in Puebla follow the example of those of Medellin. We here denounce injustices.
Our situation of a diocese that remains without a bishop since the departure of Monseigneur Nicholas greatly worries us.
We know that three priests were expelled from the country.
Bishops, know our anguish: we don't have land to work, there is disrespect for human dignity; we ask of you that this be present to all the Assembly of People.

From the Community of Santa Clara
Bishops present in the third meeting in Puebla, in the name of a group of Catholic campesinos from a rural zone of Catacamas, Olancho, Honduras, we make to them the present communication:

1. We hope that said reunion will come to aid the oppressed class of Latin America.

2. We would like that the bishops that represent Honduras commit themselves to raise a message of liberation, and with capacity to denounce such injustices that exist in our country.

3. We hope that they are going to follow farther on the agreement in Medellin, that is a Church of the people and for the people.

4. That it be a Church attached to the reality in which we live.

5. We, the depreciated class, hope that all the hierarchy be bonded with us and not with the capital.

BISHOPS OF THE III CONFERENCE OF BISHOPS
PUEBLA, MEXICA
September 18, 1978

We, the inhabitants of the community of Villa Linda, Catacamas, Olancho, Honduras, we direct ourselves to you with a brotherly greeting in the name of Christ, the Liberator, and at the same time we communicate the following:

1. We hope that in your conference the light of the Holy Spirit illuminates your hearts; that the proposed objects in the assembly be in favor of the oppressed as Christ says in Luke 4:18.

2. We hope that you give a glance to the reality of Latin America, for example: Why is there so much infant mortality, lack of medical assistance, lack of hospitals, health centers, high grade of illiteracy, bad distribution of the means of production, (the land is in the power of a few), violations of human rights, etc. . . . ? Meanwhile countless injustices occur, the government invests hundreds of millions of dollars in purchase of warlike armaments. What is the intention of these governments? Is it to annihilate the popular movements, in order to maintain the actual system? What do you think in this regards?

3. We desire that the agreements of Medellin be ratified, that our Church be a living Church that denounces the injustices that we the poor of Latin America are victim to. It is good that you abandon some of your palaces and leave for the rural zones of the

-18-

On October 30th, approximately six hundred people gathered
together from the neighboring rural areas of Catacamas to help put
up a large wooden cross over the graves of the martyrs. They
walked, carrying signs, wreaths of flowers, and small trees to be
planted around the well where the bodies had been found, arriving
shortly before nine in the morning. Immediately upon arrival they
raised the large Cross.

One of the lay leaders read the following: "It has been more
than three years now, but today, the people of Olancho make the
shame disappear. It was a shame that the Catholics in all this time
have not remembered to place a symbol that would record the gift
of self and the sacrifice of our massacred brothers and sisters at
'Los Horcones' of the valley of Lepaguare."

"The gift of: Padre Casimiro, Maria Elena Bolivar, Padre
Ivan, Ruth Garcia, Oscar Ovidio Ortiz, Bernardo Rivera, Juan
Benito Montoya, Lincoln Coleman, Roque Andrade."

"We also remember the gift of those who fell the same day in
the February 18 Center: Alejandro Figueroa, Fausto Cruz, Arnulfo
Gomez, Maximo Aguilera, Francisco Colindres."

On the cross was hung a sign with the names of the fourteen
martyrs listed and the date of their deaths. The cross had been
painted in black and red. Another lay leader read: "The red
symbolizes the spilt blood that rekindles the life of a people and
fertilizes it, a people who have to follow the example of the
martyrs in order to walk with head high. The black of the cross
symbolizes the deceptions, the lies, the repression, violence, lack
of justice that is in our country. We begin our celebration at the

113

foot of the Cross, this cross that has been planted is, and will be, for all of us and for those who see it raised on high, a reminder of the question that God asks of us: Where is your brother? The blood of your brother has arrived to me. The cross is judgment of God on a sinful world, in it the son of God, Jesus Christ, has come to know the misery of people of all times. It is for all a sign of violence, of lies, of hate, of ruin and disaster."

"But it is also the sign of Jesus who shows us love, justice, the compassion of God. It shows us that God still expects much from us, that God expects the transformation of all elements of sin, that causes death, into something that raises to life, to justice, to liberty."

"At the foot of the cross, we are going to admit our own personal sins, but also throw out the cry of supplication and weeping before the father of all the poor; the God of justice in order that he see our crushed situation and be moved to liberate us."

After a few moments of silence they continued with the Mass. Enrique preached on the story of Cain and Abel, asking, "Where is your brother?"

"For thousands of years the voice of God resounds in the face of assassins. We have come here today to crown this place that was sprinkled more than three years ago by the blood of our brothers and sisters. Our purpose is also to repeat the cry of God. To the modern Cains, we ask them, 'Where is your brother? Where is your brother, Roque? Why are you angry against him? Is it because he wants that campesinos know how to read and write?' What have they done to Juan Benito, Alejandro, Bernardo and Lincoln? Cains who don't accept that the life of your brother or sister is seen by God? The voice of the blood of Oscar, Fausto, Maximiliano, Francisco, Arnulfa, cries from this earth to God? Why don't you permit a people to raise a head lowered from so many centuries? Why do you torture and assassinate your brothers and sisters who want to change this situation of hunger and misery which is a situation of institutionalized violence?"

"The blood which cries out from the earth cries for our conversion because in one way or another we contribute today to the death of Abel. Don't let anger, envy, conformity or hatred enter into our hearts. Isn't a strong sentiment of solidarity capable of destroying all barriers and suppressing all division? Friends, what have you done to your brother?"

To Enrique's homily, Paul added, "This is an honor, a privilege, and a grace, that we are here reunited so that we can share this moment and walk on this holy land."

"They were teachers, campesinos, students, priests, people of all class and all kind, but all united in the same hope, the hope of a new world. The spirit of them remains in our people and is here present, moving among us now. Here is the spirit of Jesus, the spirit of the one who also gave his life for the people. His spirit invites us, animates all of us, in order that as our brothers and sisters, those fourteen, remained faithful, we also may remain faithful to our God, our people, our land."

During the offertory fourteen acacias were planted at the side of the well. At the end of the service, fourteen flower crowns were placed near there as well. The posters the people had carried with them were placed along the path way as they left. The people marched back in silent procession along the road, dotted on both sides with posters that remained behind.

"Cain, what have you done to your brother?"

"Many are implicated, few condemned."

"No to injustice."

"I am asking liberty, that is my cry."

"We follow their footprints."

"Let us be united."

Above all, in the distance could be seen the cross with the names of the martyrs.

Joan had attended the ceremony, traveling with Enrique. She had asked him to speak to Paul about joining them at Campamento. He did, but Paul refused to leave.

Joan was enjoying her new work with Enrique, but found that her back pain had returned despite staying off of burros. She was finding it increasingly difficult to continue her work. She hadn't wanted to leave but when her religious superior visited her and found out about her condition, it was decided she needed to return to the states for a minimum of four months, possibly longer if back surgery was deemed necessary. Paul, too, had been experiencing some problems with his back. He accompanied her back by plane to Tegucigalpa, neither able to withstand the jouncing that was part of driving in Honduras.

"Why don't you come back with me? You could use the rest."

"No, it's not that bad. Besides I've been hearing that if I leave the country, I might not be able to get back in. I'm on the list of undesirables. I have to stay. You'll come back and when you do maybe you can join me in Catacamas again."

"Maybe. Or maybe you'll finally leave your beloved Catacamas."

They didn't say goodbye when Paul dropped her off at the convent. He had been going to see her off at the airport the next day but he woke up with back spasms that made it impossible for him to go anywhere.

Joan waited as long as she could before boarding her plane, hoping to have a chance to say good bye. She turned one last time before entering the plane, looking for one last glimpse of Paul, but no luck. She would see him when she got back, she told herself as she took one last look at Honduras before the plane soared above the clouds. Little did she know that because of her work over the summer with Enrique, her name had also been added to the list of undesirables, making it impossible for her to return.

IV

"Este llamamiento nos turba y nos hace perder el sueno, porque estamos acostumbrados a vivir en el desorden que hemos llegado a llamar 'orden'… ¿Es que el evangelio esta llamado a transformar las estructuras en las que se asienta el mundo de los hombres?" (Proaño)*

"This calling disturbs us and makes us lose sleep because we are accustomed to live in the disorder that we have come to call 'order'… Is it that the gospel is a call to transform the structures in which the world of humans exists?"

-19-

What she wouldn't give for an egg over easy on dry toast. Why didn't it magically appear, or at least, why couldn't someone appear to make her request into a reality. And if he happened to be an Antonio Banderas look-alike, well, she wouldn't complain. It was precisely at that moment that Kathy decided she would remarry. Oh, not today, or any time in the near future, but some time, some random moment in the future. There were no prospect on the horizon right now, but that didn't mean he wouldn't appear when the time was right. Certainly God was preparing Mr. Right even as she lay there on her bed of sniffles. No more cold Michigan winters by herself out in the God forsaken tundra.

There were good things about where she lived. She was never at a loss for entertainment as wild critters stole into her yard

117

looking for scraps to eat. There were the raccoons that turned over her trash cans and shook them until the lids came loose, spilling waste over her yard, and the deer that ate her hostas. There was always something to see in Mother Nature's wonderland. But what good was that with no one to share it with.

This cold was the last straw: achey, fevers, chills, sore throat and cough. She had to dig her way out of her home to her driveway and drive to the college where she taught on a part-time basis. When she had been a full-time high school teacher, being sick was no major problem. She called in sick and the principal found her a sub at no expense to her. As an adjunct faculty, it was up to her to find her own sub and pay for them herself. If she cancelled class she would have to make it up, next to impossible to do. And so she tumbled out into the cold, cruel world, armed with DayQuil to get her through the day until she could collapse in her rocker recliner, covered by two afghans as she tried to stay warm in her home which she kept at a cozy 65 degrees to save on heating costs.

"If the woman at the Community Action Agency can survive keeping her home at 62, certainly we can survive at 65," she had told her son the last time he came home. This had been a running argument between them until he had joined the ranks of his siblings and gone on to college and a life of his own. There really was no reason to keep this home. It had been a great place to raise her kids, lots of open spaces and woods for them to explore, but now they were gone and she was all alone and it was time, time to move on.

She didn't have any concrete plans for remarrying, it wasn't a goal. But she hadn't ruled it out either. Better to live a happy single than part of an unhappily married couple. She just didn't want to live alone anymore. She'd settle for a friend, someone she could tolerate, who didn't talk too much or have noisy family members. Someone who would make her chicken soup when she was sick, or an egg over easy on toast.

She waddled into the kitchen, an afghan wrapped around her shoulders, put water in the tea kettle and prepared her egg, over easy just the way she liked, on dry toast. At least it was palatable as her fever raged on. She looked at the remnants of the Nyquil bottle. A lot of good that was doing her, she thought. She had never thought this miserable cold would last so long. Usually she had a fever one night then the fever broke and turned into a nasty cold. She now had three nights of fever and counting. The worse the fever, the worse the cold would be she knew from experience. This was going be one humdinger of a cold.

She wished for a bottle of whiskey. She could make a hot whiskey sling like her mom used to make then lather an old sock with Vicks vapor-rub and tie it around her neck. If nothing else it would be a comforting ritual from her childhood. When she was better, she told herself, she would buy herself some whiskey, knowing she wouldn't. She wasn't much of a whiskey drinker and didn't want to test the fates by starting now. She stuck to her glass of wine and occasional beer and left the hard stuff to others, like her former husband. Still, a little whiskey would taste good right now.

-20-

Another Holy Week. It had been so many years since Joan had been actively involved in planning Holy Week services, not since she had married. She had continued to be involved in different ways even after she had left the convent but once she had married she had other concerns to fill her time. She had drifted away from that aspect of her life. She still remembered the liturgies in Honduras, the processions. How the people had loved processions, the procession with palms on Palm Sunday, the procession with the cross on Good Friday. She remembered Holy Thursday, the washing of feet.

She remembered the ways they had tried to make the liturgies relevant to the situation of the campesinos. More relevant? How foolish of them. How could they be more relevant than they already were, those beautiful liturgies of betrayal, persecution, suffering and finally death, death of a good man who had done no wrong. Certainly they knew about betrayal and innocent lives being lost. They knew so much more about suffering than she ever did. At least while she had been there, there hadn't been the death squads like in El Salvador and other Latin American countries. There hadn't been the kidnappings, the desperacidos - the disappeared, like Columbia, Venezuela, Argentina, the cries of mothers whose children were missing, the pain of those tortured by military trained by the U.S. No, they didn't need to do anything to make Holy Week come alive for the campesinos. They lived it every day. The cross was truly in their hearts. How had she lost it?

She guessed she could blame it on Dave, but that wasn't fair. She had wanted someone stable, steady and reliable, someone to lean on through all of her ups and downs. It had been hard, coming back to the US after four years in Honduras, coming back to the middle class lifestyle of the convent here. Perhaps that had been the hardest blow, trying to fit into her community stateside when she just didn't fit. She had fit in with the sisters working overseas. She had liked living and working with those who were poor.

She didn't like the middle class environment of the motherhouse or the expressed need to get a job that paid to subsidize the ministry of the other sisters in the missions and cover the cost of the retired sisters. In essence, she had two grandmothers in the community to support. She didn't want to work so that others might have the opportunity to do what she had done. She wanted to do it herself. She had known that this was part of community, part of the sacrifice of community life; she just didn't think she could do it.

She had no longer fit in with the sisters of her community. She had changed. Where she had felt most comfortable after her return had been with the Catholic Worker community. There she found the poor of her own country. There were plenty of poor people in America, you just had to work a little harder to find them, go off the beaten path to where street people hid under bridges or in alleyways. She found herself drawn to the Catholic Workers and their lifestyle. She also was drawn to work with migrant farmworkers and the refugee population, many coming from Central America. As she fit less and less into her religious order, it eventually became apparent that it was time for her to leave. She lived with the Detroit Catholic Worker community for a while, until she found herself an apartment and a full-time job working at a refugee center.

Somehow along the way she had met Dave. Good, old Dave. He did pro-bono legal work for the refugee center. At first she had resisted his attention, but over time his good heart won her over. And then there had been two sons. She went to work for Catholic Charities, got a Masters in Social Work and then one in administration and now, here she was, an administrator in a social service agency. She would not have believed it, even though it was her life. No wonder she hated it.

How had I ended up here, she asked herself? She looked at the books on liberation theology in her bookcase, reading off the names. Gustavo Gutierez, Virgilio Elizondo, Leonidas Proaño, Ernesto Cardenal, it had been ages since she had picked up these well-worn books. She pulled out a book, *Ministers of God, Ministers of the People*. Written by Teofilo Cabestrero, it included interviews of three of the priests who had served in the Sandinista government in Nicaragua. She had remembered watching the events of that country as they unfolded, how the official Church had condemned the men. She had watched first from Honduras, then from her exile in the USA. When they had had elections in 1986, she had considered going down with others to observe the process and maybe slip over the border to Honduras. By then she figured she was no longer on the list of those banned but her children had been young. Their care plus her husband and job had absorbed all her time and energy. There was no way she could have gone then.

She flipped through the pages, stopping now and then to read parts she had underlined. She read with interest some of their comments about their own conversion experience, how the lives of the poor had changed them. She too had been changed. She read about the experience of one priest during the literacy campaign in those early years after the Sandinistas had come into power. Fernando Cardenal had related, "One fellow Jesuit of mine, a priest who'd taught me when I was in school . . . was a ham radio operator. He joined the literacy crusade with me, all fired up like a sixteen year old . . . He was in charge of the radio communications network—for all types of services and emergencies, sometimes serious, like rescuing persons in accidents, or transporting the sick or dying and then getting in touch with their families. After the crusade was over, when this priest had gone back to the school where he'd spent his whole life as a math teacher, he told me,

'Never, as long as I live, will I ever again do anything as important as that. Nothing in my life has ever given me the satisfaction that that work in the national Crusade for Literacy did.'"

Joan read it over again. That was what she was looking for, she thought, that feeling of being alive, being a part of something greater than herself, something important, life changing. Oh, to feel alive like that again. She knew what the priest had been talking about and wanted it for herself.

In contrast to Holy Week in Honduras, the celebration of Holy Week in America seemed so bland. Separated from life and death, the church seemed so stale and lifeless, removed from risk. There was something exciting about being part of a community taking risks based on faith, truly living the gospel. She wondered why she stayed, why she remained Catholic. Force of habit, maybe? But if she left, where would she go? She had wanted the stability of her faith while raising her sons, had not wanted to take risks back then. But now, what did she have to lose? What was she waiting for? Maybe it was time to once again act. Maybe it was time to take a few risks. Maybe it was time to go back to Honduras.

She walked up to the simple wooden cross being held out by the altar servers for her to kiss. She joined the line of the faithful come to venerate the cross, come to hear the words of Jesus' passion and death according to John, words read every Good Friday. She had come to hear the prayers for the church, for the world, and she had come to rededicate herself to the cross, to service. Her mind was made up. It was no longer a question of if, but when, how and how soon. She wanted to be there for the thirty-year anniversary of the martyrs, wanted to know if the people still remembered.

She couldn't go alone, knew Dave would never go along with that, but she didn't want Dave to come with her. She would have to find someone else to go with her.

"Hello."
"Kathy, hi. I'm going to Honduras and you're going with me."
"What are you talking about?"

"You have no one to keep you here. You've been complaining about wanting a change of scenery. It would give you a chance to use your Spanish. Of course you'll come."

"Are you crazy? Of course I'll come. When do we leave?"

-21-

The plan was to go on a mission trip with CFCA, the Christian Foundation for Children and Aging. Dave and she had sponsored children through them for years. CFCA encouraged sponsors to be in contact with the children and to come visit them. They had never been able to find the time to go on one of these mission trips but when she clicked on the website and saw there was one scheduled for Honduras in June, June 10-20, she decided it was perfect. She would go on the trip, get used to being in Honduras once more then go to Olancho in time for the thirty-year anniversary on June 25.

Maybe she'd see Paul again. It had been a blow when he hadn't seen her off at the airport. She found out later what had happened when he had finally sent her a letter, but that had been the end. After a short correspondence they had lost touch with each other. She wondered what he was doing, whether he was still in Honduras. How ironic that she had been the one to be banned from re-entering the country. Later, once the ban had been lifted, it had been too late. She had been too busy with her children to travel to Honduras. And so the years had passed. Good years, full years. Yet how she wished for those years back, to be young again, ready for adventure, ready to take on the world, change the world.

She wondered if any of the others she had known would still be there. Would Clemente be around? Enrique? Armand? She couldn't wait. Now that the idea had taken root in her brain and found fertile ground there was nothing to stop her. She applied for her passport, got the necessary vaccinations and counted the days.

As she prepared for her trip, she found herself drawn out of the past and into the present. What was happening in Honduras now? What was it like? She pored over any information she could find on the internet. The men who had been arrested for the

123

murders in 1975 had been released in 1980, barely five years served for the murder of fourteen. Now Manuel Zelaya, the son of one of the key players, was considering running for president. How quickly they forget. The irony of the situation was so strong. Maybe he was different from his father. Maybe he was trying to make amends. Maybe.

The statistics remained about the same. The majority of the people lived in poverty with most of the land in the hands of the wealthiest five percent. There were still massive problems with the lack of adequate health care, lack of employment, and the presence of violence everywhere. Perhaps it was even worse than when she had been there; was that possible? Mexican drug cartels had invaded the country and taken over the police so that one estimate said that thirty percent of the police were involved in the drug trade, thirty percent accepted this and forty percent threw up their hands saying, "What can I do? The problem is too big."

Kidnaping was now a common problem, so much that there was now a Committee of Relatives of the Detained and Disappeared. Just this past December twenty eight bus passengers had been indiscriminately killed while returning home to the outskirts of San Pedro Sula during rush hour, supposedly by gang leaders. She could imagine the terror on the bus, innocent men and women returning home from work, leaving children behind. The screams and tears, by those on the bus as well as by the families left behind. The fear, how would their families survive without them? How would they manage to put food on their tables? Random acts of violence putting fear into the hearts of all. No one was safe.

Gang members routinely stole money from passengers on city buses in Tegucigalpa one web-site warned her. Teens were executed, accused of gang activity or political activity. There was mistrust of the government, the police, the judicial system. In response to this there was a return to the law of the people, with private citizens taking whatever steps they felt they needed to protect themselves and their loved ones. Not so different from when she had been there.

In contrast though, she found sites that spoke of ministry within Honduras, church communities in the U.S. that had adopted

sister communities in Honduras that spoke in praise of the
Honduran people, the beauty of the country, and the rewards of
ministry with these good people. Other web-sites that describe a
different Honduras, a tourist's Mecca, with beautiful, sandy
beaches, exotic forests, Mayan ruins to explore. It was hard to sort
it all out. She suspected that the truth encompassed both realities.
That it wasn't all violence, although violence was a reality that
needed to be dealt with, just as it had been while she had been
there.

It was a mixture of both. It wasn't as bad as some reports
made out, depending on where you went and what you did. Certain
areas were more dangerous than others. She would just need to
keep her wits about her. There was continued social unrest and
attempts at organizing the campesinos with varying degrees of
success. The work went on. She searched in vain for word about
her friends. There was one way to find out.

-22-

Paul had spent a month on his back in Tegucigalpa before finally
being well enough to return to Catacamas. It had been a hard
month, although relieved some by the drugs he had been given. He
had thought about leaving, going home, but at first he didn't know
if he was even up to sitting on an airplane and when word came
back that Joan was not being allowed to return, he knew that would
be his fate as well if he left. Still he thought about leaving, or if not
leaving Honduras, leaving Catacamas. He didn't want to leave but
he was beginning to think that maybe that would be the best.

It seemed that as long as Joan was there, pressing him to
leave, he responded by resisting. Now that she was no longer
pushing him to leave, he started to think about it. What at first had
been unthinkable, became thinkable. He could join Enrique. He
liked Enrique. They could do good work together. Better to leave
Catacamas to the French. Or so he had decided during that month.
Why so stubbornly insist on staying? Maybe this was God's way
of pointing him in a new direction.

125

He returned to Catacamas with this in the back of his mind. He would tie up loose ends, say his goodbyes, then leave. He returned expecting more of the same, expecting the situation to be worse. To his surprise, not only was it not worse, Armand seemed genuinely happy to see him.

"Those sisters," he said, shaking his head, "¡Estan locas!" He warmly welcomed Paul back. The people had missed him as well. It was as if some of the problems and barriers to ministry he had been experiencing just faded away while he was gone. Or was it that he had changed? Maybe the stress and strain of the situation had caused him to see conflicts where none existed. Perhaps he had been imagining the problems. Or maybe it was a bit of both. Feeling better, more relaxed, having made up his mind to leave, it was now possible to stay. And so he had stayed.

Armand had been happy to have the help. As the lone priest, he had been responsible for all of the sacraments for the area. That meant Masses, baptisms, weddings. He was also happy because now that Paul was back, he could take a vacation. Paul contacted Enrique to let him know about the change of plans.

"I have to stay, at least until Armand returns from vacation." And so he stayed, and stayed. Clemente came back armed with his new knowledge, ready to build up Ivan's marriage preparation program again. Paul couldn't leave then. It was good to have Clemente back. Armand took this opportunity to move to another parish, leaving Clemente and Paul. Paul couldn't leave Clemente to run the parish alone, so again he stayed. It also seemed that in his time away, the people had come to appreciate him more. Absence makes the heart grow fonder, perhaps. They were more accepting, no longer constantly comparing him to Ivan. And so he stayed, and stayed, and stayed.

Every time he thought about moving, another reason came for him to stay. Even when his name had been removed from the list of undesirables and he was able to travel to the states without fear of not being able to return, even then he stayed. He visited family and friends, staying for weeks to months, but always he came back. These were his people. He had come to know them; they had become a part of his life, as much his family as his biological family. And so he stayed. Clemente moved on, but he stayed, a source of stability in a very unstable country plagued by violence and political upheavals.

He had thought about looking Joan up when he came state side, figured she was somewhere in Michigan, but by then they had already lost touch with each other. By then she had been married with a new name. So he let it go, wished her well but didn't look for her.

"Mom, what do you mean? Why are you going to Honduras again?" her youngest son had protested when he found out.

"Don't worry. You and your dad will be just fine while I'm gone."

"At least let me come with you."

"And leave your dad all alone? Who will keep him company while I'm gone? Who will call for pizza if you're not home? Besides your Aunt Kathy is coming with me. It's going to be a girls' trip. You'd be in the way."

Tim was going to be home for the summer, in between his junior and senior year. Her oldest son was away at medical school.

"Good for you, mom. I'm surprised you didn't go sooner," he had said.

Dave wasn't as equable as their oldest, yet he recognized there was no stopping his wife. His qualms were not eased by the thought of his sister going with her but he knew better than to argue with either of them. If he could get nowhere with his wife, it would be even harder with his sister. Best to let them go, armed with all the words of caution he could muster.

"Are we in trouble?" he asked.

"What do you mean?" Joan responded.

"Are we in trouble, I mean, is there anything wrong between us? Are we still okay?"

"This isn't about you. It's about me. It's just something I have to do. You understand, don't you?"

"No, but that's okay. I don't have to understand, do I?"

"I'd prefer it if you did, but, no, you don't have to understand, just let me go."

"Guess I don't have a choice."

"No, not really, but I'd rather have your support."

"That you've got. Just come home safe."

"There's nothing to worry about. It's been almost twenty years since my name has been taken off of the list. No one will remember me, besides it's a different time, thirty years later. I'm sure things have changed. If it were dangerous would CFCA be taking a tour there?"

Dave begrudgingly went along with the plan. "Maybe I should go along with you."

"Don't be silly. Someone has to stay here with Tim. Besides, you can't take that much time off of work."

"It could be arranged."

"Don't worry. I'll be fine."

-23-

The plan took shape. Kathy knew Spanish, had taught high school Spanish. Once they got to Honduras she could easily ditch her, Joan figured. Kathy would get along just fine on her own, leaving Joan free to do what she needed to do. That was her plan.

Joan packed light, one suitcase on rollers for her. She had wanted to put everything in a backpack, but her recurring problems with her back made this a bad idea. Still she wondered how useful the suitcase on rollers would be once she left the world of sidewalks and paved streets. Certainly a backpack would be better there.

Kathy had two suitcases and a carry-on bag. She wanted to be prepared for every possibility. She was happy to pay someone to carry them for her. Joan wasn't over concerned about Kathy's luggage since she wasn't planning on being with her for long. Let her worry about her own luggage. She would set her up in a nice resort where she could sit by the pool and try out the native fare until Joan came back for her.

Kathy saw the signs for CFCA being held up by the people sent to welcome their group and take them to their destination.

"There they are," she pointed them out to Joan who just kept walking as if she didn't see them. "Joan, where are you going?"

128

"Keep quiet and come with me," Joan said, pulling Kathy along with her till they got out of the airport and into a taxi.

"You didn't really want to go on that tour, did you? You'd be sleeping in homes or in barracks with few amenities."

"It wasn't really my idea of a great trip, but I thought that was the plan."

"The plan has changed. You won't tell your brother, will you?"

"That depends. What's the new plan?"

"We are going to Olancho, to Juticalpa. From there I'm going to Catacamas."

"I thought we were going to do that after the tour."

"Not enough time. Wouldn't you much rather spend the time on a beach on the Caribbean rather than be shacked up in some miserable hut with a bunch of other tourists?"

"Now you're talking. And I know just the place," Kathy started to search through her carry-on, pulling out pages of computer print-outs she had made before they left. "I brought along this information just in case the opportunity arrived. We can fly to Trujillo, spend some time there then visit one of the islands, maybe drive to La Ceiba or visit Tela. Right now there's not a lot there, which is why it's so perfect. We can get away from the tourist traps. Then we can fly back by San Pedro Sula. I've got names of hotels, restaurants, attractions, or we can just lie on the beach."

"That's fine for you, but I'm going to Catacamas."

"We can always stop there on the way back."

"No, I'm going to Catacamas. You can go on without me."

Kathy paused and asked, "So you are planning on ditching me?"

"Wouldn't you be much happier in a comfortable hotel or beach side resort?"

Kathy thought about it for a moment, lying by the pool being waited on by young Latin men. It did sound good. But no, what would her brother say if he knew she had let Joan go on alone.

"He doesn't have to know," Joan said, reading her mind.

Kathy paused again then said "No, as tempting as it sounds, I came here with you and I plan on staying with you. Maybe we can hit the beaches after Catacamas," she suggested, putting her papers back into her bag.

Joan called Dave when they reached the hotel, as she had promised. "We arrived safely but you know we'll be traveling in places without a phone available, staying with families and all. I don't know when we'll have a chance to call, so don't worry if you don't hear from us for a while, okay? Promise me you won't worry," Joan insisted, knowing it would be a promise Dave would not be able to keep, but asking anyway.

How can I not worry, Dave thought to himself after handing the phone to his son.

"Mom sounds good," Tim said as he hung up.

"Yeah," Dave mumbled.

"I still can't believe you let her go. Do you have any idea how dangerous it is in those Central American countries? Just look at the internet and see how unsafe it is."

"What are you talking about?" Dave asked.

"Don't listen to him," his eldest, home for the weekend, said. "Mom knows what she is doing. She knows the country, knows her way around. Besides she's on a tour with all those Christians. How can she get into trouble on such a tour? Don't worry about her."

Easier said than done, Dave thought.

-24-

The quickest and safest way to get to Juticalpa from Tegucigalpa was by plane, as long as their flight wasn't cancelled, which did happen at times if there weren't enough passengers. The back-up plan was to take the bus but that would have been difficult with Kathy's entire luggage. Joan arranged for the flight the next day then decided to tour Tegucigalpa.

"Ready to go out?" she asked Kathy.

"Sure thing. Where are we going?" Kathy was game for anything. She was tired from sitting on the plane and wanted a chance to stretch her legs and see the sights. She hadn't traveled all this way to sit in a motel room. She pulled some more papers out of her bag. "I've got a list of some of the local sights and a map. Where do we start?"

Joan gave the taxi driver an address. Everywhere they rode brought back a flood of memories. They stopped at the house from Joan's dreams, where she had spent those months in exile in the capital. She was relieved to see it was still standing. She asked the driver to wait while she knocked on the door to see if anyone were home. She tried to peer through the windows to see if it was the same, the same cool, white walls and rocking chairs, an oasis of peace in a troubled city. When no one came to the door she asked a woman passing by if the sisters still lived there.

"Si," she replied, "only they are gone now. They come and go."

Reluctantly Joan got back onto the taxi.

"Can we at least go to one of the places I picked out?" Kathy asked, "Or walk around the central district?"

"Sure, wherever you want," Joan agreed, lost in thought and memories.

Kathy took one look at the plane and reached for the flask she had packed in her purse. That and her rosary beads would get her through the flight, she thought. She had gotten over her reluctance about drinking whiskey, and just in time, she told herself. She had been excited about getting out of the country but the sight of guns at the airport had dulled that excitement somewhat. And now this plane…

The plane was a small charter plane Joan had managed to get seats on for them through asking the right questions and bribing the right people. Commercial airlines did not fly into Juticalpa but it was still possible to book flights on small charter flights.

Joan saw Kathy take a swig from her flask and hide it in her purse.

"It's not too late to take a flight to San Pedro Sula. There are daily commercial flights in and out of there. From there it's just a short distance to the beach."

"Oh no, you're not ditching me. I said I was going with you and I am. I'll be just fine," Kathy insisted, patting her purse.

"I thought you didn't drink anything stronger than wine."

"I don't. This is just for medicinal purposes. Besides, I'm on vacation."

"Oh, okay," Joan remarked, raising her eyebrow but letting it slide.

Joan was feeling exhilarated by being back in Honduras. Her eyes were glued to the window as she watched Tegucigalpa disappear beneath her. She leaned back for the trip, watching for any glimpse of land below. Memories came back of other flights, of that last flight with Paul, both in pain from their backs. She wondered if she would find him. Every now and then the clouds parted, revealing a lush expanse of forests and mountains. Home, she thought, it felt like home. Next to her Kathy fingered the rosary in her pocket, closing her eyes and trying to ignore the many bumps as the small plane hit air pockets. Certainly a bus wouldn't have been much bumpier, even on bad roads, Kathy thought as she fought off air sickness. Joan didn't seem to notice the bumps at all, lost in her memories.

After the plane landed, they took a taxi to a downtown hotel. Kathy was pleased to find the amenities usually associated with hotel life, air conditioning, cable TV, a restaurant and more important, a bar. They freshened up then set out to explore the plaza in the middle of the town, finishing their day at an open air restaurant for dinner and drinks.

"Tomorrow we'll rent a car and drive to Catacamas," Joan said.

"Fine," Kathy replied, sipping on her drink. "Then, if you don't find what you are looking for can we please go to the beach for the remainder of the trip?"

"No promises," Joan replied.

-25-

"Shit," Joan groaned as she pulled over to the side of the road. She had been dodging potholes the whole drive. This one appeared deceptively innocuous, being filled with water from the previous day's showers. She had neglected to slow down sufficiently and was not able to avoid it entirely, the expanse covering two thirds of the road. Bang, there had gone her tire.

"What happened?" Kathy asked.

"Stupid pot-holes. Flat tire."

"What do we do now?"

"Well, we could sit here and hope for a passing tow truck to happen by or get out and fix it ourselves," Joan said as she climbed out and looked in the trunk for a spare. Fortunately there was one, even if it was only a donut. You never knew what you would get with rentals.

Kathy climbed out and watched as Joan got out the jack and proceeded to place it under the offending tire and crank the car up. Joan attached the wrench and pulled at the lug nuts to no avail.

"Do something," she yelled at Kathy.

"Like what?"

"Give me a hand." They both grabbed the wrench and tried to pull together but banged against each other, finally falling backwards on top of each other.

"We'll never get them off," Joan remarked.

"¿Hola, que paso?" Joan was relieved to hear as a driver stopped and got out of his car to help.

"It's not a good idea," he said, "two such beautiful women alone on the road. There are kidnappers you know."

Joan ignored his comment. "Can you help us change our tire?"

"Hermana Joan?" the man asked.

"Yes," Joan said hesitantly, "and you are?"

"Juan Saucedo, you don't remember me. I was so young when you left, only eight."

"Little Juan?" Joan remembered the Saucedo family and a young urchin who used to throw rocks at her burro, spooking him and laughing.

"Si, from Culmi."

"What are you doing here?"

"I work in Catacamas now. I've got a good job. I own a groceria."

"Good for you, Juan. I'm happy for you."

"See, here are my children, four of them. They all go to school at Catacamas. They are going to go to the university when they are old enough. Here is Juan Jr. He is going to take over the store from me. The girls will be teachers and little Pedro, he will be a doctor or lawyer. And here is my wife." Juan proceeded to pull pictures out of his wallet.

Kathy interrupted, "That's nice, but do you think you can help us here?"

"Oh, sorry, no problem, anything for Sister Joan."

"I'm not sister anymore."

"You will always be Sister Joan, riding on her burro, giving us candy. I always remembered you," Juan said as he easily undid the nuts and replaced the tire. "This tire, not good. I'll follow you to Catacamas. I know someone who can get you a good deal on a tire," he said as he finished up. "I knew you would come back."

Joan smiled, "And how did you know that?"

"Because of the saying, don't you remember, 'Olancho es ancho para entrar y angosto para salir,' - Olancho is wide to enter and narrow to leave."

"I don't remember that one. I found it quite the opposite. Olancho was easy to get out of but hard to get back into. Didn't you know I wasn't allowed back into Honduras? That's why I didn't come back."

"Oh, I remember that, but that was long ago. What took you so long?"

"Long story."

"But you are here now. It won't be so easy to leave," he said with a smile.

"What was that about being hard to get out of Olancho?" Kathy asked as they were back on the road, dutifully being followed by Juan.

"Just a saying. It just means once you get Olancho in your heart, you can never leave."

"Oh," Kathy said suspiciously, not completely believing her.

"Well, there are some who would say it means once you get in you can't get out. Others say, 'Olancho: Entre si quiere, salga si puede" – that is, "Enter if you want, leave if you can.' But that was from before, back when there was more violence. I prefer my version."

Kathy wasn't reassured by this.

Joan had thought about going back to Juticalpa to the rental place to get the tire but didn't want to lose another day. She wanted to get to Catacamas before the afternoon rain showers so she continued to Catacamas and paid for a used tire from Juan's brother-in-law.

"We are all family here," Juan said with a gap-toothed grin.

"Thank you, Juan," Joan was anxious to see the church and ask about Paul but wanted to get settled into their room first. There had been only one hotel with a pool in Catacamas. Joan had suggested this one to Kathy, thinking she would enjoy sitting by the pool, but when Kathy saw there was no bar on site, she vetoed the decision. Besides the look of the pool had been questionable and other amenities were lacking, such as air conditioning. Kathy did not envision herself spending any time at it. They decided on Hotel Juan Carlos, checked in, unpacked and settled into their room before the afternoon deluge. During the rainy season there was rain every day, but usually the showers weren't long and served to clear the air of dust. Not like the hurricanes that appeared later in August and September. June was definitely a good time to visit.

Now that she was here and settled in, the urgency to see Paul suddenly left her, replaced by a reluctant anxiety. What was she thinking? What if he were not here? What if she came all this way for nothing? What if he was gone, or worse, what if he was dead? She had been afraid to ask Juan about him. Afraid of what he might say. She tried to stop these random thoughts from running through her head. She reminded herself that Paul wasn't the only reason she had made this trip. There were plenty of other reasons, but right now he was foremost in her mind. She was having a hard time getting him out.

They enjoyed a leisurely meal and walked around the area of the hotel before calling it a night.

"So when am I going to meet those friends of yours?" Kathy asked.

"Tomorrow, tomorrow will be soon enough," Joan said as Kathy drifted off to sleep.

Joan slept restlessly all night, waking up periodically, unsure where she was, feeling lost. It had felt so good to be back in

Honduras but now that she was in Catacamas she was beset by
doubts. Had this been a foolish idea? What will Dave say when he
finds out, if he finds out, no when he finds out. She couldn't keep
something like this from him forever, could she? It had all been a
mistake. She never should have come. She'll stop by the rectory,
find he's gone and then be on her way. She was way too old for
such games, she told herself. She decided the sooner she got this
over, the better. She would go first thing tomorrow morning. But
then they had to have breakfast and Juan stopped by, anxious to
see how she was doing and eager to show her his groceria.

"They all want to meet you. You must have lunch with my
family," he had insisted, so there went the morning. And then it
was too hot. Time for a siesta and the afternoon rain. They walked
to the open air markets, enjoying the view of the mountains then
walked the Mirador de la Cruz, a pathway leading up to a large
white cross that looked over the city and before she knew it
another day had gone by. This is crazy, she told herself, but she
had enjoyed meeting Juan's family.

"We've got to check out these caves," Kathy insisted the next
morning. "And then market street. There were so many bargains.
We have to shop again."

"Okay," Joan agreed, relieved for another excuse to avoid
stopping by the rectory.

After three days, she was determined to go. She wanted to go
alone but Kathy insisted on coming along.

She knocked at the very familiar door and was surprised when
a priest answered rather than a housekeeper. She gazed at the priest
for a few minutes before saying, "Clemente?"

"Si, and you are . . .?"

"Joan, don't you remember me?" He looked at her with
confusion.

"Joan? It's been so long. I never would have known it was
you."

"But I knew it was you." He still had his Latin good looks
even if thirty years later. His hair was flecked with grey and he was
heavier but there was no mistaking that good natured smile. She
gave him a hug.

"And who is this?" Kathy asked, pushing forward.

"Clemente, this is Kathy, Kathy, Father Clemente," Joan said with an emphasis on father.

"Father, what a shame. Any more like you around?" she inquired.

"I have two brothers, both of them lawyers."

"Married?" Kathy asked. Joan interrupted before he could answer.

"So, Clemente, are you still here at Catacamas?"

"No, I'm at Juticalpa right now. I came for the meeting. We are planning a memorial Mass for June 25, followed by a March on Tegucigalpa. Paul's one of the organizers.

"So Paul's still here?" Joan asked nonchalantly, despite her heart being in her throat.

"There's no moving him from St. Francis. He's the immovable force," Clemente said with a laugh. "Everyone else moves around him and he stays. He's in the meeting. Do you want me to get him?"

"No, don't interrupt the meeting. Can I sit in?"

"This way," Clemente said as he led the two Americans to the meeting room.

"It shouldn't be too much longer," he whispered as he showed them to seats in the back of the room.

Joan soaked it all in, so many memories, so little change. So much like when she had left, she thought. Paul hadn't made many changes over the years. He had been a creature of habit, she remembered. She glanced at the room predominately filled with men, all dressed in jeans and dress shirts. In the middle was Paul. There was no mistaking him. His hair was greying, his face tanned and leathered from the sun and the years, his thin frame had bulked up over the years, but it was still him. The same voice rattled off Spanish with ease. She wondered if he would remember her. If he had seen her come in, he showed no sign of it as the meeting continued. She caught bits and pieces from where she sat. Kathy also scanned the room with interest.

She watched Paul, so like himself, listening then jumping in with a comment, summing up and moving the discussion. There was a map of the area posted to one side which they referred to now and then in their planning, mapping out the direction of the march. She began to get drawn into the planning. They were planning a protest march. It was a mixed group of priest, religious and lay leaders. The idea was to honor the martyrs by completing what they had not been able to do thirty years ago. Even though the two priests and the women had had nothing to do with the plan for the march which had given the landowners the excuse they wanted to round them up and murder them, it was felt by honoring the peasants who had died, they would also be honoring the others.

Religious leaders were joining with local political and civic leaders to pull this off. There was concern expressed within the group about being part of this larger political movement. They would have less control and be open to being infiltrated by people coming just to stir up trouble. Some of the group wanted them to stick to the Memorial Mass and not join the march because of this. There also was concern about local police and military preventing the march and using it as an excuse to jail local leaders. Paul acknowledged these concerns but encouraged them to go forward with their plans. Despite the concerns they decided to step out in faith and participate as planned.

By the conclusion of the meeting she was on board as well and anxious to participate. Kathy had long since lost interest, tapping her food impatiently as she waited to get out. As the meeting broke she leaned over and said, "Can we go now?" Joan ignored her, waiting for the room to clear out enough so she could speak to Paul. Finally there was just Paul, Clemente and another man left in the room. She walked forward to make her presence known.

Clemente saw her and interrupted the conversation to alert Paul to her presence.

"Paul, you remember Sister Joan," he said. Paul turned around in surprise then smiled.

"Joan, of course I remember Sister Joan," he said as he extended his hand in greeting. "What brings you to Catacamas?"

Joan resisted the urge to say you, knowing full well how foolish that would be. She smiled, took his hand and said, "I couldn't stay away forever. Just visiting old friends. Oh, and it's no longer sister."

"We'll have to get together some time. Maybe dinner," he said then proceeded to return to his conversation. Joan had not come so far to be ignored.

"How about lunch today?" she insisted.

Paul turned back around and paused, "I'm afraid you caught me at a bad time. We've got so much to do."

"Nonsense," Clemente broke in. "Please join us for lunch. We could use the break." He invited both of them.

"We need to work out details," Paul said with some resistance.

"We can do that after lunch. We need a break from all this planning. Company for lunch would be a welcome diversion."

"All right," he said, "suit yourself. Stay for lunch."

"Thank you. Happy to do so," Joan wasn't about to miss the opportunity. She wasn't to be dismissed so easily. The third man was Clemente's brother, Santiago, the lawyer. He seemed very happy about the diversion.

"We can always talk business. We don't always have an opportunity to have lunch with such pretty guests."

Clemente, Santiago and Kathy kept up the conversation during lunch. Paul was preoccupied. Joan asked him what was wrong.

"I'm sorry. I'm being rude. I'm just distracted. Nothing's wrong, it's just there's so much to do before the twenty-fifth. My mind is full of details."

"Tell me about it."

"It won't interest you. You want to talk about old times."

"Won't interest me," Joan said shaking her head. "How little you know me," she added. When he looked perplexed she explained. "I'm not just here to reminisce. I'm here for the anniversary of the martyrs. I want to help. I don't want to just be an observer. Fill me in. Is there anything I can do?"

At that Paul began to talk about the plans, what had been done, what needs to be done. Joan listened intently in order to figure out what she could do. This was what she had come for, she told herself. This is why she was here. It was clear to her now. It wasn't about visiting old friends. It wasn't about a vacation. It was to take part in this.

As Paul talked it was as if thirty years had not passed. They were working together just as if she had never left. They fell back into an easy pattern of relating. Meanwhile Kathy and Santiago were hitting it off as he told her about all the local sites.

"Have you visited the caves yet?" he asked.

"Yes, we went yesterday."

"Well, you haven't truly seen them till you've seen them with me." Joan made plans to meet Paul at the rectory the next day while Kathy made plans with Santiago.

-26-

What was he thinking, Dave asked himself as the plane lifted off from Detroit Metro airport. What indeed. Joan would probably not be happy to see him. He knew that. He had spoken to her just a few days ago and she had been fine. In fact, she had been better than fine. She had sounded . . . happy, alive, happier than she had been for a while. Why couldn't he make her that happy, he wondered?

She had only talked for a few minutes, just long enough to assure him that she was fine. She would be home by the end of the month. There was no need to fly to Honduras to check up on her. He could hear her already. But then her mom had fallen and broken her hip. It wasn't an emergency. She was in the hospital under the watchful eye of her sister. Still he knew she would want to know. He had called the number for CFCA to find out how he could get in touch with Joan only to be told she had never arrived.

"What do you mean? She's in Honduras. I just talked to her the other day."

"I'm sorry. She never showed up at the airport. We thought she had changed her mind. We don't have a policy of checking up on adults who sign up for our tours. Kathy Johnson didn't show up either. I'm sorry I can't help you."

He had felt like such a fool. He should have known. How like Joan to sneak off on her own. She knew he would never have let her go off alone, would have insisted on coming with her, hence the subterfuge. So if he knew she didn't want him along, what was he doing now? And that sister of his. A lot of good it had done to

140

send her along. He should have known Kathy would be no help to him. She's probably lounging on a beach somewhere while he stayed home and worried. So why was he inconveniencing himself for them?

Maybe because while lounging on a beach sounded like Kathy, it didn't sound like Joan. She was so responsible. He would have been okay with them spending the time together at some resort on the Caribbean, although he would have wanted to join them. No, if that had been the plan, Joan would have told him. Something else was going on.

Joan had called on their home phone rather than his cell so he didn't have the phone number that she had called from. He called the phone company and requested the number. When he called he got the front desk for a hotel in Catacamas, Honduras. He asked if a Joan Johnson was registered.

"Si, along with a Ms. Kathy Johnson. Did you want me to connect you to her room?"

"No, that's fine. Thank you," he said as he hung up. If she had wanted to cover her tracks she would have signed in under a fake name. Moments later he was on the internet, booking a flight to Honduras. Fortunately he had a current passport because of business travel he had done overseas now and then. His high school Spanish wasn't entirely gone as he had Spanish speaking clients at times. They usually had an interpreter still he could manage a small amount of conversation. Enough to get by, he hoped.

"You're doing what?" his son asked.

"Going to Honduras to find your mom."

"You are crazier than she is. How are you going to get around? You don't even know the language."

"I know enough. Besides I know where she is staying. I just need enough Spanish to get there. How hard can that be?"

"If you know where she's staying, why don't you just call her?"

"No, it's better this way," he had insisted. He knew what Joan would say if he called. She would have insisted that she was fine and not to worry about her. Now he was wondering whether maybe that would have been the smarter course. He could have called. At least then she would have known he knew. He could have at least gotten some accounting of her whereabouts, what she was doing, that she was okay. But no, something compelled him to go and see for himself what she was doing, that she was okay. He hastily made arrangements to take some personal time from work, packed one bag, his briefcase and a Spanish-English dictionary and was ready to go.

When his son tried to come along he insisted he stay home.

"You need the money from your summer job for school, besides who would take care of the dog." Tim reluctantly agreed.

So here he was, on his way to Tegucigalpa, the capital of Honduras, via Miami. He had packed light. He had a briefcase full of legal briefs he had planned on reviewing during the flight. The briefcase remained unopened as he stared out the window. He had taken an early morning flight which got him into Tegucigalpa by early afternoon. From there he took the bus to Juticalpa where he would stay overnight before taking another bus to Catacamas. He wanted to have a good night's sleep before seeing Joan, wanted to be refreshed and in good form when they talked, not worn out from travel and lack of sleep. Not that he would sleep well. He had not been sleeping well since he found out she was not with the tour. At least this way he had the possibility of sleep.

The flight had been uneventful. The bus ride, while crowded, hot and bumpy, had been relatively uneventful as well. He had been surprised at how well he slept, perhaps because of the lack of sleep the last few days. Perhaps because he felt better already just knowing how close he was and that he was actually doing something rather than staying at home feeling helpless. After all of the hours of sitting, he had collapsed onto his bed and slept until woken by the sun.

He felt peaceful and at ease, until he remembered where he was. Yesterday seemed like a dream. He couldn't possibly be in Honduras, and yet here he was. Now that he was here he was even less certain what to say than before he had left. He tried rehearsing his dialogue. He would be calm and unconcerned. He wouldn't let her see how worried he was. That would only annoy her.

He remembered what she had been like when they had first met, so strong, so dedicated. He had liked that in her. After twenty five years of marriage he sometimes wished she wasn't so strong, so resourceful, that she would lean on him now and then instead of being so stubbornly independent. A guy liked to feel needed sometimes, needed to feel like he was at least somewhat important, that he wasn't superfluous. Funny how what attracted you to a person at first can become a stumbling block later. He had been attracted to her independence back then, admired her. Now he just wished she were a little less independent, at least where he was concerned.

He checked out of his motel room and took the morning bus to Catacamas. Another hot, noisy, bumpy ride. He regretted bringing his briefcase. What had he been thinking? That maybe he would have some free time to stay caught up on his work? That he didn't want to waste any time? He knew what he had been thinking. He had considered renting a locker at the airport and picking it up on the way home, but no, maybe he would have some time to get some work done so he lugged it along with him. He had also considered cramming it into his suitcase. He had packed light, but not that light. Two pairs of khaki pants and a pair of dress slacks, just in case, several short sleeve shirts and some polo shirts filled the suitcase. He hadn't brought a suit jacket. Didn't foresee any need for that, but did stick a tie in. You never knew when you would need a tie. Add socks, underwear, shaving supplies and he was packed.

The bus let him off not too far from the hotel. He decided to go ahead and rent a room. He figured either way it would be needed. If he was in the dog house for coming, he would need it. If not, then Kathy would need a room. This was easier than finding out what room was Joan's, seeing if she was there and waiting around for her if she wasn't. The desk clerk smiled as he signed in, "Ah, you are here for las señoras Johnson?"

Dave didn't respond. He was on his way to his room when he caught sight of what he believed to be his sister. She was sitting out on the patio, sipping a drink and talking to some man. Her face had been covered by a large hat and sun glasses but there was no mistaking her voice.

"Kathy?" he said as he approached.

"Dave!" Kathy said in surprise. "What are you doing here?"

"I might ask the same. And who are you?" Dave asked the man.

"This is Santiago. He's been showing me around."

"I'm sure he has," Dave muttered. "I need to talk to you," he said, taking her by the shoulder, "alone."

"You can talk in front of Santiago." Kathy pulled him closer to her, "don't worry. I'm not doing him," she added.

"Where's Joan?" Dave asked.

"Hermana Joan?" Santiago broke in, "She's at the rectory, where she is every day." Dave did not like the sound of this.

"Relax, Dave, sit down, have a drink. You're not in America anymore," Kathy said as she pulled out a chair for him.

"I don't want a drink. I want to talk to you, alone. And since when do you drink?"

Kathy made her excuses to Santiago and stepped aside with Dave.

"That was rude," she said.

"Rude, you call that rude. How about disappearing from the face of the earth and not letting me know? And who is this Santiago? And what is Joan doing at the rectory?"

"Take it easy, counselor. One question at a time. We didn't disappear. We've been in Honduras the whole time. We were coming home at the end of the month. And Santiago is just a friend. Nothing's going on. Besides, he's married. He's just showing me around while he's here in Catacamas on business."

"What business does a married man have showing you around?"

"Long story. Why don't you go up to our room?"

"I've got my own room."

"Fine, why don't you go up to your own room, put these bags away and join us for lunch?"

"I'm not hungry. You didn't tell me why Joan is at the rectory. What is going on?"

"That's for Joan to tell you, but don't worry, it's nothing," Kathy said with some hesitation which only made Dave all the more worried. He went up to his room, left his suitcase on the floor, freshened up then went back to the patio. He didn't want to unpack till he knew where he would be staying.

"Where is the rectory?"

"By the church, of course. Didn't you see it as you drove through?"

"I wasn't exactly sight-seeing." Kathy gave him directions.

"If you would just wait until we are done here, we'll take you." Dave didn't want to wait around, especially not with Santiago.

"I'll find it," he muttered as he set off, clutching the paper with directions, showing himself to clearly be a tourist, if there had been any doubt. He found his way to the church, then to what he believed to be the rectory and paused before getting up his nerve to knock. What would he see? Some Latin priest spending time with his wife? He didn't want to go there. Kathy had said it was nothing. Since when did he believe anything Kathy said? Not since they were kids and she had tricked him one too many times and got him in trouble with their parents. He knew better. She would say what she thought she had to say to get away with whatever it was they were doing. He composed himself and knocked on the door.

"¿Buscando Señora Johnson?" he asked the elderly woman who answered the door, using his limited Spanish. "I was told she was here."

"Ah, Hermana Joan," the woman said with a smile. "Si," she continued in rapid Spanish that Dave didn't understand. He knew enough to know she wanted him to follow her.

She led him to a room and indicated that Joan was there. "Gracias," he said as he peered into the room, unsure what he would see or what he should do.

There was a meeting going on. Several men and in the middle of them was Joan, intently focusing on the conversation, joining in with ease, pointing at something on the table and making notations at times. No one saw him come in. The housekeeper hadn't announced him but had left him to make his own introductions. So he was able to watch quietly and try to get his bearings. Clearly they were planning something but what he didn't know. Joan looked great. So at ease, tanned and relaxed despite the intensity of the conversation. There were three men with her. One was American, although his speech didn't give him away as he rattled off Spanish. The other two were Honduran.

He took a step through the door and attempted to break into the conversation, not sure what to say, but also feeling it wrong of him to observe without letting anyone know he was there.

One of the men saw him and interrupted the others.

"¿Que paso?" the man said and started towards Dave. Joan looked up, "Dave?" she said.

"Who is he?" another asked, clearly unhappy about the intrusion.

"That's Dave, my husband," Joan said, still not sure she was seeing right.

"Your husband, why didn't you say so," the American got up and offered a firm handshake, "I'm Paul, Fr. Paul. Your wife and I worked together in Honduras many years ago. It's great to have her back, so nice of you to share her with us." Dave just stood there, not saying a word, unsure what to say, staring at Joan as she got up as well. Paul caught the look between them.

"I'm sure you have a lot to talk about," he said. "We were just about finished. We can break for lunch," Paul said and hurried the other men out of the room.

"Nice to meet you," he shook Dave's hand again as he made his retreat.

"Hola," he said sheepishly as Joan approached.

"What are you doing here?" There was no smile, no hello, but she also wasn't yelling. That was promising, Dave thought.

"Your mother broke her hip. I thought you would want to know."

"You came all this way to tell me that?"

"Well, you didn't exactly leave me a phone number or address."

"But you found out where I was. You could have just as easily called me. Why are you here?"

"Are you kidding? Why am I here? Why shouldn't I be here? You are my wife, off doing God knows what."

"Yes, God knows what I'm doing."

"You know what I mean. I was worried about you. I knew if I called you would have told me not to worry and not to come."

"If you knew that, why did you come?"

"Here we go again. Isn't it enough that I am here? So what are you doing? You and these men?"

"Those men happen to be priests."

"So."

"So, there's nothing to concern you."

"Then tell me what you are doing."

Joan realized she had to tell him the truth. She paused, walked back to the table, then said, with her back to him, "We are planning a Memorial Service in memory of the martyrs. You knew about that. I told you I wanted to be here for the thirtieth anniversary."

"Is that all?" Dave started.

Joan interrupted, "And we are taking part in a mass demonstration against the current government."

"Oh," Dave paused as he let this sink in. That didn't seem so bad, not as bad as the worst case scenario he had played in his head. "Well, good, I mean that doesn't sound so bad. Why all the secrecy?"

"You mean you're okay with this? You're not going to insist I leave?"

"When have I ever been able to keep you from doing something that was important to you? When have I even tried? You know I've always been one of your biggest supporters."

Joan broke into a big smile, "I should have known I could count on you. So you are not going to try to stop me," she said incredulously.

"Why should I?"

"I'm so glad to see you," she said and hugged him. "I was sure you would say it was too dangerous. I should have known better."

"Of course, you know you can count on me," Dave said with relief now that she was in his arms. Then he stopped and pulled back.

"Dangerous? What do you mean dangerous?"

"Oh, it's nothing, it's just, well, you know, organizing demonstrations here are somewhat different from in the U.S. We can talk about it over lunch," she said and pulled him along.

-27-

She woke in the darkened room. For a moment she couldn't remember where she was. She turned over and bumped against a warm body. She hadn't, had she? But she had, it all came back to her. What was she doing here, in this room, with this man? She quietly slipped out of bed, hoping to slip out of the room and out of his life when he awoke.

"Where are you going?" he asked sleepily.

"Ah . . . to my room?"

"This is your room, silly," he responded.

"Oh, so it is."

"Come back to bed." He patted the warm spot she had just vacated. Kathy slipped back into bed as quietly as she had slipped out. He pulled her close while her brain raced. What am I doing, she thought? He gently kissed her and nuzzled the back of her neck. Oh hell, she thought, I'm going to hell but . . . who cares. She relaxed into his arms and went back to sleep.

When she woke again, this time he was the one slipping off quietly.

"Where are you going?" she asked.

"I have to get to work. Unlike someone I know, I'm not on vacation. I still have to work. Go back to sleep, my Katerina," he said as he leaned over to kiss her. "Meet me for lunch?"

"Mmmm," she mumbled through the kiss. "Yes," she said as he left.

She was confused, not exactly sure how it all had happened. It had seemed so, well, not exactly innocent to start with, just a fun flirtation. Isn't that what she had wanted, a dalliance with a Latin lover? It had seemed so fun, mildly wicked and enticing, but she had not thought it would go this far. He was married after all. What was she thinking? What about his wife? And his children? Did he even have children? He had avoided any mention of any of them. Doesn't mean they don't exist, just that he was hiding something.

So what's the problem? They were two adults doing what consenting adults did. No harm. His family didn't need to know anything about her. Soon she would be flying home where she would forget all about him. It will just be a sweet memory. Something to hold onto during the cold of winter, the memory that once, just this once, she had been wild and crazy instead of so responsible. The memory of an affair, a love that will not be tarnished in her memory but that will remain sweet, untainted by reality and the ravages of time. What was so bad about that? She rationalized as she got up to begin her day.

She would meet him for lunch, maybe have a few more such luscious nights together, or maybe an afternoon encounter, then she would leave. No one need know, except of course, her brother and Joan, but they could be sworn to secrecy. What good would it do them to blurt out her secret? So she had determined her course of action for the day. She enjoyed her breakfast then sat by the patio waiting for her lunch rendezvous.

That was where Dave found her. He sat down next to her.

"So, enjoying yourself?" he asked.

"What do you mean?" she snapped at him.

Taken aback by her response he said, "Nothing. Just an innocent question, a conversation starter. Just wondering. Catacamas isn't exactly the great tourist destination. Thought maybe you would be bored by now and ready to go to an Oceanside resort."

"It's all right. I'm finding things to occupy my time."

"Or finding someone, like that lawyer you were with yesterday?"

"Yes, now that you mention it, it is nice to have someone to talk to while Joan is off saving the world."

"I appreciate you staying here with her when I'm sure you would much rather be somewhere else. Now that I'm here, you don't have to stay if you don't want to."

"And who would keep you company while Joan did her thing?"

"Oh, I brought along some work."

"That will not do, little brother. You can't spend all your time holed up in your hotel room working. When was the last time you had a vacation?" she paused as he tried to come up with a response.

"Just what I thought, way too long. You are the one who should go to the resort, but, of course, you won't. At least let

Santiago and me show you around and keep you company if your
wife won't. You can talk lawyer talk all you want."

"I don't want to impose. Besides, I might be able to help Joan
some."

"Yes, and how did that work for you?"

Dave thought back to the previous afternoon, sitting in on a
meeting where he understood nothing, had nothing to contribute
since his use of the language was so limited. At least he had got to
spend time with Joan but it wasn't exactly how he had wanted to
spend his time and Joan knew it. He had enjoyed having lunch
with her and then dinner with her and her priest friends who had
struggled to include him in the conversation by speaking English,
but then there had been yet another meeting before Joan was done
for the night. A string of never-ending meetings, he never would
have stayed, would have tried to talk Joan into leaving, except that
she seemed so happy, so alive. He couldn't bring himself to intrude
on her happiness. After all, this was her adventure. He had
imposed himself into this part of her life. He was relieved to accept
her suggestion that he stay at the hotel this morning and had fully
intended to get some work done but instead was lured to the patio
where he had found Kathy.

"So, how is everything going between you two?" Kathy
asked.

"Fine, just fine, why do you ask?"

"Just wondering. Not every husband would be so okay with
his wife sneaking off on a tropical vacation and spending so much
time with those men."

"Not every wife is Joan and those men happen to be priests."

"They are still men."

"Who are you to talk, you and this Santiago?"

"Touché. Maybe better not to discuss either situation."

"No, actually it's okay. I'm not quite sure what to think. Joan
is so happy here. Do you think I'm losing her? Not to those men,
but to this country? It seems she has found something here I can't
give her, something she needs. I don't know what to do. I can't
compete with it, whatever it is. I just know I want to be here, in
case, just in case, she might need me. Is that pathetic?"

"Not at all, big brother. You sound like a husband who loves his wife. It's sweet. I wouldn't worry. Joan will come around. She is just enjoying herself right now. It's all so new and different, exciting, overpowering," Kathy said, perhaps more to herself than to Dave. Was she talking about Joan or herself? She shook her head from her reverie about Santiago. "I'm sure she is fine," she reassured him.

"I hope so," Dave said in agreement while inside he wondered.

"Hey, enough serious talk. We are on vacation. How about a Bloody Mary? Put that briefcase away," Kathy suggested.

"That's all right. I think I will get some work done before lunch. Do you want to join Joan and me?"

"I'm meeting Santiago," she said. Dave left her to her own thoughts, pre-occupied with his.

He was pleased when Joan announced she had the afternoon off. She showed him around the city, sharing stories, memories from long ago. It was good to have her to himself for a while. They returned early to their room where they made love then napped until dinner.

"Can't you stay longer?" he asked when she prepared to leave for more meetings.

"Can't, the celebration is in just a few days. There is so much that needs to be done."

"Then at least let me help. There must be something I can do. I don't want to just sit around doing nothing while you work. Let me be a part of this."

Joan reluctantly agreed to have him tag along. She put him at the table where people were signing in and picking up assignments then proceeded with her meeting.

There were a lot of details to take care of, not just for the Memorial Mass, but for the march. They were coordinating efforts with others throughout the country. Arrangements had to be made for transportation for those who couldn't walk, water and food supplies provided along the way, press releases sent out, message control and non-violence trainings for all participants as well as providing security lest some try to infiltrate their group and stir up trouble as had happened during the March for Water two summers ago. Then the government had sent people to stir up the crowd and give the military an excuse to turn a peaceful demonstration into a violent one. A small group of trouble makers can cause a lot of harm. The government controlled the media and had focused on the violence rather than the thousands of peaceful protestors and their message. They were doing everything in their power to keep this from happening again, including the trainings in non-violence for participants and their own security forces trained to intervene non-violently at the first sign of trouble.

And then there were the details for the Mass. They were going to meet in Juticalpa on Friday, June 24; the Memorial was to be early the next morning, six a.m. in order to have time to walk to the site of the massacre, Los Horcones ranch outside of Lepaguare. They had debated about having the Memorial Mass at the actual site. There were many concerns about holding the Mass outdoors, many logistical concerns as well as security concerns. Armed gun men protected the site, keeping people from trespassing. It would have been a challenge to pull this off. They had been in negotiations with Manuel Zelaya, Jr., about allowing them access to the actual site but in the end decided it would put too many people at risk. They would get as close to the actual site as they could, spend some time in prayer and then spend the night in Limones.

The plan was to walk twenty to twenty-five miles a day for three days, arriving at the outskirts of Tegucigalpa on Monday, June 27, in order to walk the final distance through the capital to the square for the demonstration at noon on the 28th. Joan had poured over the maps along with the rest of them, looking for good locations to stop along the way, preferably where there was a Catholic church or a community center that would be willing to provide shelter if needed. Where this was unavailable they would sleep under the stars, hoping for rain-free nights as they had limited tents, also calling upon the good will of those they encountered for possible floor space, use of toilets and extra water to supplement that which they would be carrying in the trucks.

Joan helped with the planning for the Mass, preparing readers and scheduling Eucharistic Ministers to distribute communion to those who would attend. Music had to be selected, the church decorated, banners displayed, some of which they would carry in procession to Los Horcones. Joan was focusing her attention on this. It felt good to be planning this liturgy. After the Mass the march would begin. On their way to the capital they would be joined by others; peasants from all over Honduras would gather in the capital on June 28. It was a huge undertaking.

Paul was definitely in his element as he made plans, put out press releases, spoke on the radio himself encouraging all to join in the effort, and speaking with other leaders. He was so much more confident and assured of himself, comfortable in his surroundings than thirty years ago. It was a confidence that comes with age and experience. Yet in other ways he was still the same. Thirty years had passed and yet it felt like yesterday they had been planning that last Memorial Mass. Joan was relieved to see some of the other organizers take Dave under their wings, putting him to work so that she was free to do her work. As the evening wore on, they invited him to join them in a few cervazas, beers. It gave her the opportunity to speak with Paul as they finished up some details.

They sat down together as Paul broke out two cervezas.

"Why didn't you come back?" he asked her.

"You know why. I wasn't allowed back. Besides, I did come back. It just took me a long time."

"No, you know what I mean. The need is so great here. We needed help, always need help. Why didn't you return once you were able?" The question had been nagging at him for years. He had understood at first when she hadn't come back. She couldn't. He had accepted that and gone on with his ministry. When years passed and her name was finally removed from the list of those not allowed in the country, he had somehow thought she would come back but she didn't. Still he hadn't given it too much conscious thought. There was too much to do to wonder about lost opportunities. It had been pushed back into the recesses of his mind. But now that she was back the question had come into the foreground.

"Don't you think I've asked myself that same question, over and over again, over the past twenty seven years? I don't know. Just never seemed to be the right time. I was busy about so many responsibilities. And then there was Dave . . ."

"Yes, Dave," Paul interrupted. They both looked over to where he was drinking with a group of men. For some reason Paul had never imagined Joan as married.

"Yes, Dave. He's a good man. He truly is. And then the boys."

"You have children?"

"Didn't I tell you? One is in Med school, the other in college, still not sure what he will do with his life."

"Like his mother," Paul said with a smile.

"What do you mean?" Joan asked.

"You are still searching, aren't you?"

"Does anyone ever stop searching in this life? Isn't that to stop living? 'And the end of all our searching will be to reach the place where we started and recognize it for the first time,' as T.S. Eliot said."

"Or, as Augustine said, 'Our hearts will not be at rest, till they rest in thee.'"

Joan smiled, "So yes, I am still searching. Do we ever stop?"

"It's good to have you back, Joan. Any chance your searching might lead you to stay here? We could use you. You have already been a tremendous help. There wouldn't be much pay but you would have an opportunity to make such a difference." The question had slipped out before he even knew it and now it couldn't be taken back. Perhaps more important, he didn't want to take it back. Now that he had said it, he realized he meant it. He had missed her over the past twenty some years, more than he had allowed himself to recognize.

"Are you saying I'm not making a difference where I'm at, with what I'm doing?"

"No, I don't mean that. I'm sure wherever you are, you are making a difference. You can't help but do that. It is your nature. I didn't mean to offend you. I apologize if I did."

"No offense taken. You haven't said anything I haven't asked myself countless times over the years. I have missed this country."

"It does get into your blood. So stay. Your kids are grown. They can get along without you."

"And Dave?"

"He's a grown man. He can decide for himself." They both looked over at him again. "He seems to be getting along just fine. We can find work for him too. Could always use a good lawyer. I'm sure it could be worked out."

"I'll think about it," Joan said. "Time to call it a night," she added as she finished off her beer. "See you tomorrow."

She gathered Dave from his new found friends and they walked back to the hotel.

What had he been thinking, Paul asked himself as he watched Joan and Dave leave. She was married. He had no business suggesting that she leave everything she had built in the states, her job, her sons, her husband, in order to return to Honduras. He had no money to support another ministry position. And even if he had, wouldn't it be better to use it to hire one of the campesinos who were a part of his church already and so desperately needed the money? Still, it had slipped out. He hadn't planned it, it just happened.

It had been so nice, having her back, working with her again. It was like old times. He had regained something he had lost, his youth. Oh, to be young again, ready to take on corruption in the government, in the church, ready to set the world on fire. Somehow, with Joan back, all of that seemed possible again. His back didn't ache quite so much, there was a spring in his step that hadn't been there since . . ., he didn't know when.

"Saw you talking to Sr. Joan tonight. What about?" Clemente asked.

"I asked her to consider coming back," he responded.

"You what?"

"I asked her about coming back to Honduras, what's the harm in that?"

"In case you didn't notice, she does have a husband."

"I'm not trying to sleep with her. We could use her expertise. There's so much work yet to be done here."

"You are treading in dangerous waters, amigo."

"What are you talking about? Besides, she hasn't said yes yet, just that she would think about it."

"Why put yourself and her in a potentially compromising situation? She is no longer Sr. Joan."

"But I'm still Father Paul, nothing will happen."

"Just a warning. Better men than us have fallen when given too much opportunity," Clemente said before going to his room. Both were all too aware of the number of men who had left the priesthood over the years, often the best and the brightest. Paul was all too aware of the challenges of celibacy. He had dealt with that in the past, had made his choice and would stick with it. So why did it keep raising its ugly head?

"What were you and Paul talking about so intently?" Dave asked.

"I didn't think you had noticed. You seemed to be having a good time with Manuel and the others."

"I was but that doesn't mean I was oblivious to everything else. What new scheme were you coming up with?"

"Paul wants me to stay and work here."

"Out of the question. Did you remind him you have a job already, and a home and responsibilities?"

"I told him I'd think about it."

"What?!" Dave stopped and faced her. "You'd think about it? What is there to think about?" This was precisely what Dave most feared only hadn't been able to voice. "What about me? Our sons?"

"The boys will manage. You can manage too. It's not impossible. Besides, I didn't say yes, just that I would think about it. Can't we even talk about this?"

"No," even as he said it, Dave regretted it. He knew it was the beer speaking. He knew it was the wrong thing to say but it had already been said. He couldn't take it back. "No, I won't have it. It's too dangerous. It's okay for a visit, for a few weeks, but to move here, make it permanent? How could you do that?"

"Well, I guess if you have any say about it I can't. It's a good thing it's not up to you," Joan said and walked away from him.

Dave hurried after her, aware that he had blown it. He had always been supportive of her in the past, why couldn't he be supportive now? But this was different, so different. How could he let her go, but if he didn't, maybe he would lose her forever. Either way, he would lose her.

"Joan," he caught up with her, tears of anger and frustration were on her cheeks. "I'm sorry, of course we can talk about this. I just don't want to lose you."

"Maybe you already have," Joan said.

"No, don't say that, not now, not yet, we can work this out if this is what you want to do. We can talk about it."

"I don't know what I want to do. I just know I have felt more alive these past few weeks than I have for the past twenty-seven years, since I left here. I've never felt quite right since I left. Now that I'm here again, I don't know what I think."

"It's stressful. You've been working so hard. Now is probably not the time to talk about this. There's still so much to do before the 25th. You'll be able to think more clearly after all this is done. Then we can talk more."

"Maybe. Maybe you're right. Now is not the time to make any decisions. I just need to know we can talk about this."

"And that we can, just not tonight." They both agreed as they walked back. They didn't talk about it. It remained unspoken yet very much present between them.

Dave and Joan got up the next day after a fitful sleep and went back to the rectory and their respective jobs. Dave was happy to have something to occupy his time while allowing him to be around Joan. Joan was happy that Dave was occupied.

-28-

It's just a meaningless fling, she kept telling herself. "Isn't that precisely what I had been longing for, a Latin lover named Julio, only in this case his name was Santiago," Kathy reminded herself. So then why did she feel so guilty? The only problem was that Julio had a wife. Never in her imagination had she dreamed of a pool boy with a wife. He had always been conveniently unencumbered with responsibilities. That was part of the appeal. Clearly his wife just wasn't satisfying him, or maybe she was insane, locked away somewhere in an asylum and he, being the

157

noble man he is, refused to divorce her. He never talked about his wife or any of his family, but, of course, why would he? It was just a casual fling, some fun that would be a sweet memory when she returned home.

Still, he was married. What was she doing? This was not her. She had never planned on it going this far. It was going to be a harmless flirtation. Then Dave showed up, Joan moved into his room, leaving her all alone in her hotel room, defenseless, and next thing she knew they were in bed together. It was Dave's fault, she told herself. If he had minded his own business and stayed away, she never would have been so tempted. No, it was Joan's fault. She never should have moved out leaving her so vulnerable. She didn't have to sleep in the same room with her husband. That would have shown him, showing up like that out of the blue. No fair warning. Certainly she could find someone to blame besides herself! It was Santiago's fault, taking advantage of a lonely divorcee. At least he had the opportunity for all the sex he wanted. He could have satiated his appetite with his wife. But then, boys will be boys, as the saying goes. "No, I won't let him off the hook so easily," she told herself.

She had finally decided to break it off that afternoon, over lunch, but then he had been so sweet. He had brought her flowers and told her how beautiful she looked and she was ready to go back to her room with him, if only he hadn't had to go back to work. "What was a quickie among friends," she thought, then in the same voice retorted, "How can you be so weak?" How could she be? She didn't know. So then she went back to saying it was a harmless fling. It would be over and done with and she would be gone. No harm done.

"What do you tell your wife when you are gone overnight?" Kathy asked the next morning.

"She knows my business often keeps me away, but let's not talk of her," Santiago said, leaning down to plant a kiss on her lips while she sat in bed.

"No, I want to know about her. Tell me that she is grossly overweight, unappealing, not interested in sex, or incapable of orgasm. Anything to make me feel better about this," she demanded.

"No, she is a lovely woman. We have just grown apart."

"Do you have any children?"

"Enough. I have to go. Will I see you later?"

"I don't know," Kathy said, unsure of herself.

He leaned over and kissed her again. "That is a promise. A promise of more to come," he said as he left.

What should I do? How did it get so complicated? I need to talk to someone, Kathy thought, but Joan is unavailable. Darn her for being so busy when I need her. I can't talk to Dave about this. He would just tell me I had to break it off, that I had been foolish to let it get so far. Who else? A priest? Surely I can't talk to Clemente, his brother. And Fr. Paul thinks of nothing but his big march to save the world. But in confession, perhaps if I went to confession, they couldn't tell anyone. But what would they tell me that I don't already know myself. That it is wrong, sleeping with a married man. It is wrong to sleep with anyone you aren't married to.

Kathy decided to go for a walk before meeting Joan and Dave for lunch. She browsed through the market looking at fresh fruit, hats, clothes. She had seen it all before. Today's trip wasn't for shopping, just thinking, until time for lunch.

"They are running late so they asked me to keep you company until they get here." She had been surprised by Clemente, sitting down in the chair next to her. At first when she had heard his voice she had thought it was Santiago. "How are you enjoying your stay in Catacamas?"

"Just fine. It's a lovely town, the people are so friendly," she gave the rote answer. They sat in an awkward silence. Finally she decided to ask, "So Father, tell me about your family. Do you have any more brothers besides Santiago?" She had no idea what Santiago may have told him so thought it best to play it safe.

"Yes, I have one other brother, also a lawyer, and three sisters. Six children total in my family."

They continued with small talk, are you the oldest? What do your siblings do? Then Kathy asked, "And tell me about Santiago's wife. He speaks so little about her. Do they have any children?"

"His wife," Clemente said with a puzzled expression. He
paused then asked, "What has he told you?"

"Very little."

"That's interesting," he said just as Dave and Joan joined
them, changing the conversation.

Damn, Kathy thought as Dave and Joan arrived, rotten timing.
She made up her mind. She would break it off tonight after dinner.

And that is what she intended to do, but then they had drinks,
and then they went for a walk in the moonlight.

"Aren't you worried about someone seeing us together and
telling your wife?"

"Oh, no, I live too far from here, on a secluded ranch. My
wife doesn't get many visitors. She likes it that way."

"Oh," Kathy said, preparing her next words carefully, when
Santiago's phone rang. He looked at the numbers and said, "I have
to take this." There were a few words exchanged before he hung
up. "I'm sorry. I have to go. Something has come up. I'll be gone
for a few days. I'm so sorry."

And at that point, so was she. What would she do over the
next few days? At least he had provided her with some diversion.
"But will I see you again?" she asked, forgetting she had ever
considered breaking up.

"Ah, si, I wouldn't let you leave without seeing you. It will
just be a day or two. I promise." With that he kissed her, walked
her back to her hotel and left.

All for the best, she had told herself. It had to end anyway.
Maybe it's just as well it happened this way. Still she had wanted
to be the one to break it off. How unsatisfying to have it happen
this way. She decided that she wouldn't sit around pining after him
but would finally do what she had been planning on doing all along
– she would go to the beach. She caught Dave and Joan at
breakfast.

"I'm going to take the bus to Juticalpa and fly to La Ceiba for
a few days."

"Are you crazy?" Dave said. "It's not safe. I can't have you on
that bus by yourself, and do you know where to go in Juticalpa? At
least tell me Santiago is going with you." Despite his urgings that
she go to the beach when he first got here, now that it was an

impending reality he was beset with brotherly concern. Besides, then he had known so little about travel in Honduras. Now that he knew more, he was no longer ready to let his little sister go off on her own. If he had known what he knew now before he had come, perhaps he would not have gotten on that flight from Detroit. Sometimes ignorance is bliss.

"No, he's not, in fact it's over between us. You are both so busy. I don't want to just sit around here by myself."

"Dave, you can drive her to the airport in Juticalpa," Joan said, "At least let Dave drive you."

"Oh, okay," Kathy agreed.

"She'll be all right," Joan insisted. "Her Spanish is excellent. I'll check on hotels that are safe. Just keep your wits about you," Joan warned. "Don't do anything foolish."

"Like sleeping with the pool boy," Kathy said.

"You said it, not me," Joan smiled.

"I think I've had enough excitement for one trip. Sleeping on the beach is all I'm looking for now."

Dave gave them both a look of consternation, then realizing he was out-voted, gave in. He did not want to leave, but given the situation he could see this might be the best solution.

"But then what are we going to do about getting our luggage back to Tegucigalpa?" The tentative plan had been for Kathy and Santiago to drive back with all of their luggage while they took a small bag with them on the march.

"We can work that out," Joan assured them. "Right now Kathy's safety is what's most important."

The drive to Juticalpa was uneventful.

Dave finally broke the uncomfortable silence. "So, you okay?"

"No, but I will be."

"It was doomed from the start, you know."

"I know, big brother."

"Little brother. You know you're the older one."

"You were born older than me. You've always been the more responsible one, the fair-haired boy, the lawyer. I'm the screw-up."

"You were daddy's girl."

"A lot of good that did me. Doesn't seem to have helped me where men are concerned." Dave didn't know how to respond to that.

"So, how about you?" Kathy asked.

"Me, I'm fine."

"Are you really? Come on counselor, I can recognize a lie. I've told enough of them in my life."

"No, maybe I'm not so golden after all. Twenty-five years of marriage and now this. I feel like Joan is slipping away. I'm losing her to this country."

"It is a beautiful country."

"A lot of help you are."

"Sorry, I'm afraid I'm not one to advise about marriage."

"Joan's so independent. I appreciated that in her when we first met. I loved her spirit of independence and her concern for those who were lost, alone, abandoned in the world. Now it seems that it's precisely those things that are taking her away from me."

"She does love you. I know that."

"But is it enough? She's always been so driven by her causes. I may be losing her to a cause." They drove the rest of the way in silence, one they mutually agreed to without saying a word.

By the time they made it to the airport the only flight to Trujillo had already left. From Trujillo Kathy would take the bus to LaCeiba.

"Don't worry," Kathy told him. "I'll get a room for the night and get a flight tomorrow."

"Are you sure? I don't feel right about leaving you here alone."

"I'll be fine. My Spanish is better than yours. If anyone should be worried, I should be worried about you. You better get on the road to Catacamas before it gets too late."

Dave dropped her off at a hotel then headed back to Catacamas.

Santiago had been anxious to get back to see Kathy. Their time together was so limited, he didn't want to lose any of it. He drove home and tied up loose ends as quickly as possible in order to be free to come back the next night. He was surprised to hear she had checked out.

He hunted down Joan at the parish center who told him her plans. Dave arrived as they talked and filled him in.

"You left her to fly to Trujillo by herself?" he asked in disbelief.

"She's a grown woman, fluent in Spanish. It's a tourist resort town. She'll be fine," Joan reassured him, but that wasn't the problem. How could she have left without him, without saying goodbye? He hopped in his car, hoping to make it to Juticalpa before it was too dark.

Kathy tossed and turned once in bed. Somehow it had seemed like a better idea last night. She had slept well since making a decision to leave, but now she wasn't so sure. Was she running away? Yes, she was, but what reason did she have to stay? It would have been foolish. Time for her to get on with her vacation and her life, maybe meet that unencumbered pool boy, no, wait, she had had enough of that. But Santiago, he had been so sweet. Now he would just be a sweet memory. After all last night had just been a taste of what a relationship with him would hold, making excuses to go back and be with his wife, just as he made excuses to be with her. That was not how she wanted to live.

She was surprised to hear a knock at her door. She hadn't ordered room service. She got up out of bed, threw on a bathrobe and went to the door.

"Who is it?" she asked.

"It's me, Santiago, let me in."

She cracked the door and saw it was him. "What are you doing here? I thought you were going to be gone for a few days?"

"I was able to take care of the matter more quickly than I had thought. Please, let me in."

Kathy paused, then opened the door the rest of the way. He tried to kiss her but Kathy raised her hand, stopping him. "Explain yourself," she said.

"Me, explain myself. What have I to explain? I told you I would be back. You are the one who left without saying goodbye. You owe me an explanation."

"Look, Santiago. I just can't do this. I can't be involved with a married man. It's been fun. I really like you, but it's not me. I can't do it anymore. I'm not that person."

"What person?"

"You know, the other woman, the home breaker."

"Would it make a difference if I told you I am not married?"

"What? What are you talking about? Yes, it would make a difference, but that is not the case. You are married and we are through."

"But what if I wasn't married?"

"Not possible. You told me you were married. You've got some explaining to do."

"I know. I know it was wrong. Please listen to me."

"You're not married?" Kathy asked again, not quite grasping what he had said. "Get out, get out," she stated then added in the same breathe, "Why did you lie to me?"

"I know, please listen to me," Santiago pleaded. When she remained silent he continued. "My wife is gone, she died two years ago. I saw you and thought, what a beautiful woman, but I didn't want a relationship. I didn't think I was ready. You seemed safe. You were only going to be here for a few weeks so I thought, why not? Why not enjoy some female companionship, no strings attached. I thought by saying I was married it would be safer. We both would know it wasn't going anywhere. Just some fun. But then I think I may love you. I don't want it to just be a fling," he paused to give Kathy a chance to respond.

Kathy didn't know what to say. Finally she asked, "But what was the emergency? Why did you have to leave?"

"My little girl, she had fallen off her horse. They were sending for the doctor. I didn't want to leave you but my little girl, I had to."

"Of course you had to. Is she all right?"

"Yes, just the wind knocked out of her and a sprain, but she's okay. Nothing broken. I would love for you to meet her."

"But," Kathy was still trying to get her mind around the fact that he wasn't married. "But, I don't want anything serious. I didn't want anything serious. I just wanted a fling too. I have to leave in a week. What then? I have to go home."

"We can work it out."

"No," Kathy said as Santiago started to kiss her. "I don't want to get serious about anyone. I don't want to be in love. I . . ." her protests were muffled by his kiss.

"I can't wait for you to meet my daughters and see my ranch," he said softly as he caressed the small of her back and gently kissed her.

Kathy drove back to Catacamas with Santiago the next day. He took her to stay at his ranch where she met his daughters, one twelve the other eight, their nanny and the rest of his staff. They wanted to spend as much time as they could together, knowing the time was limited.

-30-

It had been several days and still neither of them had brought up the unanswered question. Joan tried to put it out of her mind in order to focus on what needed to be done. For Dave it was ever present, much though he wanted to forget it. He watched Joan from his distance, wondering at how happy she seemed to be. They had meals together, sometimes alone, sometimes with others. People kept coming from outlying areas. Priest, religious, lay leader packed every bed and eventually every floor space. Dave was grateful for their hotel and the modicum of privacy it provided. He wasn't as sure about Joan. She reluctantly left the church each night but even she was aware that she needed the rest and comfort a bed provided. Her fifty plus body could no longer easily tolerate sleeping on hard cots or the floor, so she came back to their room each night however reluctantly. He insisted on breakfast together before going back to their organizing efforts. At the church there was a festive, party-like atmosphere as people gathered, old friends met, new friendships were created.

Paul was reveling in the excitement, even with the possibility of violence, the danger to himself as one of the leaders, perhaps because of it. Joan watched him and marveled. He calmly recognized threats against his life as just part of life here, not ignoring them completely, yet not letting them influence his decisions. He seemed to thrive on risk, to come more alive the greater the danger. Not her, she thought. Paul for his part, watched her out of the corner of his eyes. He smiled when he caught her eyes on him but wouldn't return her gaze, trying to focus on the work at hand.

There had been much discussion months ago about the nature of the events. Some in the religious community had wanted to keep it strictly a religious event of prayer and fasting, not involving secular groups. The advantage of this was greater crowd control and message control. The minute you invited secular groups you ran a greater risk of violent elements taking over what was meant to be a peaceful protest. Because it was the thirtieth anniversary Paul along with others had held forth for a broader coalition, inviting in different community organizations in hopes of having a greater impact.

The March Against Hunger was meant to be a time of prayer as well as protest against policies that hurt the poor. The idea was for people from all walks of life to join in prayer for their country and those in positions of power. Members of secular organizations were instructed about the intent and asked to respect the atmosphere of prayer, but just how this would play out in reality was unknown. Walkers would be encouraged to sing hymns along the way, to pray the rosary or silently pray as they walked. Those coming from Olancho felt well prepared. How other communities were handling their preparation was yet to be seen.

Ready or not, though, the time was at hand. Dave and Joan joined in the parade of people going from Catacamas to Juticalpa, buses, trucks full of people. The people were to sleep in the church, on the floors of the community center, wherever they found a piece of floor. They drove back in the rental car Joan had leased weeks ago. Dave had made reservations at a hotel to give them one last night of sleep in a bed before the walk. Joan had been reluctant to leave the group but had been convinced by both Dave and Paul that it was in the best interest of all that she get a good night's sleep.

"You've done all you can do. Go, get a nice dinner and some sleep. You will need it in the days to come," Paul had insisted. Dave dropped her off at the hotel with their one small piece of luggage. Once again Joan lamented not bringing a backpack. That would have been much easier to carry. Their luggage was going by truck along with other supplies for the trip, food, water, blankets for sleeping. The remainder of their luggage they had left with Kathy to bring back. As earlier planned, she was going to drive from Catacamas with Santiago on the last day of their march. They were going to meet at the hotel where Dave had made reservations then fly home the next day.

Dave had been happy to make the arrangements. It gave him something to do to help him feel useful. He knew if he had left it up to Joan, she'd be sleeping on the floor of that church. That would not be good for her or him with their soft American bodies. Not like the peasants who weren't used to the luxury of soft beds and hot and cold running water. She had begrudgingly agreed to the arrangements, but had to admit she appreciated having a bed to sleep in and a shower to wash off in after the hot day.

Dave returned the rental car then joined her. They enjoyed dinner in the hotel restaurant, neither spoke much, both lost in their own thoughts. When finished, Dave didn't want to go to their room yet. He was feeling restless.

"You go on up," he told Joan. "I'll be up shortly. Just want to stretch my legs, maybe get a drink." He escorted her to the elevator, then went to the bar for a drink. While nursing his drink, a man sat down next to him and struck up a conversation in a heavily accented English. He seemed anxious to work on his English.

"You are far from home. What brings you to our fair country?"

Dave was reluctant to talk. "Just visiting," he said.

"So you have friends here?"

"You might say that."

"Are you here for the activities tomorrow?" Dave shrugged his shoulders and gave a non-committal grunt, hoping to be left alone, however his interest had been aroused.

"Me, I'm a cop, brought in for extra security for the day."

"You expect trouble?" he asked, trying to seem not interested.

"Always a possibility. These people, they just won't let it rest. Every year they do something to stir up the people. A Memorial Mass, processions, they make a lot of noise and then they go home. Nothing changes. Every year, the local police have to bring in extra police to guard against rioting. It costs the community. Good deal for me. I get paid over-time. Not so good for the community. Who pays for our time? Not my concern." He took another swig from his drink. "Best you avoid the area around the church and the march. Go to the market, see the sights. Stay away from downtown."

"And if I go?"

"Up to you. I can't guarantee your safety. Do so at your own risk. Who are these friends you are visiting? If they were real friends they would tell you to stay away."

"Fr. Paul," Dave decided to give him that bit of information in hope of getting more back.

"Fr. Paul, crazy gringo. Better not to have anything to do with him."

"Why is that?"

"He is well known, well liked, even respected, but he has crazy ideas. He stirs up the people, to what avail? What good does it do? Better he say his Masses and stick to his prayers, leave the government to us."

"But isn't the government for the people?" Dave asked.

"Crazy gringo with crazy ideas. This isn't America. You and other gringos, you come to our country with your charities, stay for two weeks and think you know us, know what we need, how to help us. If you really want to help, go back to your country and do something there. Look at your own government and policies that promote injustices here. Then maybe you can talk to me about Honduras and our problems." With that he finished his drink and got up to leave. "I hope I don't see you tomorrow," he said as he left.

Dave left shortly afterwards. He didn't necessarily disagree
with what the man had said. Perhaps better to work for change in
his own country. But how to get Joan to see this, he wondered. He
chose not to say anything about the conversation to Joan when he
went back to their room and joined her in bed.

"Everything all right?" she asked as she turned over.

"Sure, fine."

"Better get some sleep. It's going to be an early morning," she
muttered and laid her head back down.

-31-

The Memorial Mass went well. Along the way to the site of the
massacre people sang hymns and prayed the rosary, appealing to
the Virgen de Suyapa to hear their calls. Other times they walked
in silence, carrying large red banners, announcing "the blood of the
martyrs" and "even the stones will cry out."

It was a peaceful, prayerful, uneventful day. There had been
some tension as they approached the site of the massacre. They
went as far as they could before being stopped by the soldiers.
They said their prayers then returned down the road.

Dave and Joan had walked in silence that first day. What was
there to say? Each was lost in their thoughts. Periodically they
would take turns riding in the trucks to give their legs a rest.
Neither was used to walking such a long distance, especially in the
heat. Dave had to push Joan to ride in the truck. She resisted but
was grateful when she recognized how hard the walking was on
her aching muscles. Riding in the truck wasn't exactly ideal either
though, bouncing and jouncing along, putting pressure on her back.
It was a relief to get out again and walk. Casual conversation was
exchanged with the other walkers. For the most part the silence
was a relief. It was a relief to be able to be lost in her thoughts.

Joan thought about the events of the past few weeks. She also
found her thoughts going back to her home in the states, her sons,
her family, her work. She was missing them. Was this what God
was calling her to, she asked herself? Was this to be the next phase
in her life? And if so, what of her marriage? She knew of other

169

couples that had survived periods of living apart, but she also knew it was hard. Is it possible God could be calling her to this ministry even if it meant the end of her marriage? Could that possibly be God's plan? Certainly, if this was what God was calling her to do, somehow the marriage part would work out too, wouldn't it? She didn't know. She looked over at Dave, carrying on a halting conversation with a woman walking alongside of them. He was being such a good sport about everything. She smiled at him and he smiled back.

It was definitely tempting, joining in the struggle of these people. Yet for all this hard work, all that had been done, she saw so much that hadn't changed. What needed to happen for real change to take place? She didn't know. But more important, where was God calling her? That she also didn't know.

She had gone along with Dave in the plans for their last few days here. Even if she were to decide to work here, she would still have to go home, take care of loose ends. She knew that.

Dave had been relieved when Joan made no fuss about the flight home. He thought that was a positive sign. At least she wasn't going to abandon him entirely without some fore thought and forewarning. His thoughts wandered to his work, the work he had brought with him, undone in his briefcase. He pushed it out of his mind in order to focus on the events around him. His Spanish was already improving as he listened to the conversations of those around him. He was even able to carry on a halting conversation with some of the walkers. He liked these people, this country. Would he ever be able to make a home here, he asked himself. So simple – their lives were so simple in comparison to the life he had left. Maybe that was what was attracting Joan. Maybe.

They slept fairly well that night, tired from the day's walk. They had been among the fortunate few to have an air mattress to sleep on. Again Joan had resisted this small comfort but been grateful for Dave's insistence as she lay on this luxury. Dave had wanted to see if he could book hotels along the way. This she had refused, wanting to be with the people and share their experiences as much as her body would allow. As it was there were very few hotels along the road and their chance of stopping in their vicinity was not very good. They slept on the floor of the church in Limone along with the others.

She was stiff the next day, but not as stiff as she had thought she might be. She was psychologically prepared for the journey if not as physically prepared as she had wanted. She was managing much better than she had thought possible. It was the right time, the right place, all was falling together she told herself, despite all of her worries to the contrary. Dave was also holding up surprisingly well, she thought, and Paul … well, Paul was Paul. Being the priest, he had a bed in the rectory with the other priests. Others had insisted on this as well. It just wouldn't have been proper for him to share the floor with everyone else. And that was okay. Paul made up for it by walking all the more, encouraging every one with his smile, kind words and jokes, at times leading singing in his off-key voice. So far so good.

And what about Paul? Joan watched him as he walked up and down the side of the procession. He was oblivious to her existence as always, not that she expected anything. Still, it would be nice to know she meant something more to him than just another "worker" for justice. She had no right to expect anything more from him, no more than she had thirty years ago, still it would be nice, she thought. Some things don't change.

There were two more long days ahead. They started with Mass at the crack of dawn then began the second leg of the journey. They hoped to reach El Rosario Laja Picada by night fall. The next day they would get to the outskirts of Tegucigalpa in order to be in town by noon for the demonstration. As they walked, more people joined them, swelling their ranks as well as straining their limited resources. Yet each new group brought additional supplies so that none went hungry at lunch or dinner, as the miracles of the loaves and fishes unfolded in their midst. They had enough for everyone and leftovers for the next day.

The number of police patrolling the roads also increased. Paul would stop and chat with them periodically as they drove by in patrol cars, forcing the walkers further to the side of the road. He invited them to share in their meal. A few took him up on his offer, easily mingling with the walkers. Others kept their distance lest this compromise their ability to do what must be done, banging heads in the event of violence.

The closer they got to their destination and the more people who joined, the more the tension increased. Still the second day was uneventful and relaxed, as was the third day of the journey. Dave and Joan were developing an easy rhythm of walking together, talking, and not talking, just being together. Joan was glad for Dave's company. They awoke, increasingly sore and stiff each morning. Joan was both anxious and excited about what the journey would hold. Dave was mostly anxious. The anxiety was put aside during the morning Mass and breakfast. Theirs was a diverse group, not all Catholics, yet all were welcome at the Mass. Those who didn't attend still respected the time and kept the noise to a minimum.

Each morning started out well with a festive atmosphere which quickly quieted in the miles yet to go. The closer they got to the capital, the more people joined in as well as increasing traffic as busses full of workers who were headed to the rally passed them, forcing them off the road and on to the uneven side of the road. Lunch was quickly eaten in order to make good time. When they reached the final leg of their journey, they pitched their last camp and enjoyed a fiesta, finishing off much of their remaining food, leaving just enough for breakfast the next day and a light lunch for those who would be returning by bus. People were singing, celebrating throughout the evening, gathering around campfires and chatting long into the night.

Dave and Joan called it a night early, leaving the campfire for others. They cuddled for warmth and fell into a restless sleep, awaking at dawn with the sound of the cock crowing. The rest of the camp was late getting up, not having to be at the rally until noon. They celebrated Mass at nine, cleaned up the camp sight and prepared to leave by eleven. The streets of the city had been cordoned off by the police for the walkers. They walked with ease through the streets. The atmosphere was light as some sang, others chanted, "the people united will never be defeated."

It was a challenge to remain with their original group as so many had joined and walkers from other parts of the country converged on the city. Dave and Joan were able to stay together but soon lost sight of Paul and many others from their group. They were but a small part of this larger mass of people.

They crowded into the square and attempted to listen to the speakers. It was difficult to hear even with the sound system because of the size of the crowd, doubly hard for Dave to understand the Spanish. The crowd cheered. Dave asked what was going on.

"I'm not sure," she said. Then there was the sound of angry shouting to their left as someone seemed to be disrupting the gathering. The sound of what seemed to be car backfire or gun shots was heard.

"What's going on?" Dave asked again.

"I don't know. We have to stay calm," Joan tried to calm those around them as people began to shout, "They are shooting at the crowds."

The people around them, who moments ago had pushed to be in the square, were now pushing to get out.

"Don't panic," Joan shouted. "It's just a few trouble makers, remain calm." Her voice was drowned out by the crowd.

The speakers on the platform noticed the altercations and also encouraged them to remain calm as the police tried to break up the group causing the problems.

As the people around them surged to get out of the square and away from the police, Dave grabbed Joan and pulled her away along with the rest of the crowd.

"We've got to get out of here," he said.

"No, we have to be calm," she insisted.

"No, we have to leave." He grabbed her by the waist and almost picked her up in his effort to get her out of harm's way. She finally realized he was right and ran with him down a side street. Once the police had cleared the area where there had been trouble, Joan wanted to go back to the rally however it was already breaking up. The crowds were moving away, claiming victory because of the success of the rally and the numbers in attendance, others simply complaining of empty stomachs. It was an anticlimactic end to a long anticipated event.

Dave and Joan found the rest of their group back at the meeting place after most of the crowd had dispersed. They picked up their suitcase and prepared to go to their hotel. Others had already climbed in the busses that had been provided for their return to Olancho. The sounds of singing and conversation poured out of the windows.

Apparently it had only been a small group involved in the altercation with the police. It had been unfortunate that it had happened so close to where they had been standing. Paul was standing amongst others from their group chatting about the day's events. He had been on the platform with the other key leaders and was pleased about how everything had worked out.

"I'm going to be staying in the capital for a few days so we can review the day and make plans. Do you want to join us tonight?" Paul asked. "We'll be watching the coverage on TV, checking out other media and releasing our own information to the press."

Joan hesitated and looked at Dave before responding. "I'll let you know. We are supposed to have dinner with Dave's sister tonight," she said as Dave picked up their suitcase and proceeded to the hotel.

Paul watched her walk away, momentarily distracted from the job at hand. It seemed she was walking out of his life. He wanted to call her to come back but knew he had no right to do so. She had never been his to start with. In the meantime, there was work to do, he reminded himself. He could always lose himself in his work.

Joan looked about the hotel room then sat on the bed and removed her shoes and prepared to hop in the shower. After the events of the last few days, it was a relief to wash away the layers of sweat and grime from the road and then collapse in a bed with clean sheets.

They turned on the TV to see if there was any news coverage of the rally. Much to their dismay the media chose to focus on the small group of trouble makers and ignore the message of the thousands who had gathered peacefully.

"Typical," Joan muttered. "I'm sure Paul's furious."

"Did you want to go over there?" Dave asked. "See what's happening?"

"All I want to do is take a nap," she responded. "Wake me up for dinner." Dave turned off the TV and joined her in her nap.

Kathy and Santiago arrived at the hotel shortly before six p.m. They had planned their drive to avoid the marchers as much as possible. They passed busses and walkers going in the opposite direction but for the most part the roads had been passable. They settled into their room and called Dave and Joan's room, waking them up.

"What time do you want to meet for dinner?" Kathy asked.

"What time is it?" Dave responded as he looked at his watch. "How about seven? We can meet in the lobby."

"Seven o'clock," Kathy told Santiago. "That gives us time for a quick shower."

"Time for a something else," he said as he put his arms around her waist and smiled.

-32-

Their flight was scheduled to leave at noon. That gave Joan just enough time to say goodbye to Paul before going to the airport.

"Do you want me to go with you?" Dave asked.

"No, this is something I want to do myself. You go ahead with Kathy and Santiago. I'll meet you at the airport."

"What are you going to tell him?"

Joan paused and thought before responding. "I'm not sure," she responded. She had gone over the situation in her head repeatedly the last few days, having ample opportunity to reflect over the course of the long walk. But she had come to no conclusion. One minute she was sure she would stay; the next she was equally sure she wouldn't. She tried out each scenario in her mind, trying to get a feel for what it would be like, how it felt, was there a sense of peace in one choice to help her discern? She got nothing.

"Wait for the light," she remembered one spiritual director from her youth telling her. "When in darkness, wait for the light." But she couldn't wait forever, could she? How long was she to be in darkness? Still she could make no decision. She thought maybe

175

she should return home and then make up her mind. So that was her tentative plan.

Dave had been afraid to let her go. He feared he wouldn't see her again. That she'd decide to stay in Honduras and not show up at the airport. But she wouldn't do that. She would at least show up to tell him goodbye, he reassured himself. She would at least go home, see their sons, say goodbye to friends, wrap up stuff at work, before taking such a step. She would at least do that, he told himself again.

"Joan, wait," Dave stopped her and took her hands. "You know I'm just a lawyer. I don't know a whole lot about all of this religious stuff, but it seems to me, where you live, what you do, doesn't matter. What matters is that you are doing what God wants you to do. I've seen how you've been this last week, how happy and alive." He looked away from her for a moment and took a breath, afraid he wouldn't be able to say what he wanted to say. "If you feel that this is where God is calling you, then do it. We'll work it out somehow. Whether I take early retirement and join you or we live apart for a while, travelling back and forth as we are able, we can work it out. If God is in this, it will all work out for the best. We'll work it out, just so we do it together."

Joan paused then said, "You know I dream about Honduras, about being here."

"Good dreams?"

"No, nightmares. I keep remembering . . ." she paused before proceeding. "I feel like I abandoned the people, especially the children. Honduras does stay in your heart, but not always in a good way."

"But you had no choice."

"Maybe at first, but later, I could have come back."

"But then what about our children?"

"I know, I don't know what I think. Maybe I should have gone back even at the risk of my life, maybe I'm the one who should have died. Why did I live? Why did I escape to my comfortable life when so many others didn't have that option?"

Dave remained silent. He had no words. What could he say?

"I've got to go," Joan said before letting go of his hands and slipping out the door. Joan took a taxi to the rectory where Paul and the other priests and religious were staying. She was glad for the few moments alone with her thoughts. Paul was finishing breakfast while poring over the morning paper and muttering. Joan smiled when she saw him and suddenly she had her answer. It was clear to her now.

"Joan," he said with a smile, getting up to greet her. "We missed you last night. Glad to see you today. I was worried you might slip away without saying goodbye."

"I wouldn't do that. You should know that."

"Sit down. Have you had breakfast yet?"

"Yes, I ate at the hotel. I only have a few minutes. I have to meet Dave and Kathy at the airport by eleven."

Joan sat down. "So," she said, not quite sure how to start.

"So," Paul repeated, "have you thought more about coming back to work in Olancho."

"Yes, I have," Joan paused, "I'm afraid I have to say no."

"Maybe you need more time to think about it. I wouldn't expect you to start right away. Talk it over with Dave, give notice at work," he said.

"No, I don't need to think it over. My life is there, in the States, with Dave and my family and my work. It was good to come back here, good to visit. I needed that. But now it's time for me to go home." Joan stood up, preparing to leave.

"I'm disappointed, but I'm not surprised," Paul said as he stood up. "Don't be a stranger this time, don't wait another thirty years to visit. It's been wonderful having you here. I will miss you," Paul added. They exchanged glances, not quite sure what to say next. Joan was surprised by this admission of feeling from Paul. Perhaps he had changed, perhaps the years had mellowed him, she thought momentarily.

"You don't be a stranger either, at least you could email me now and then. Let me know what's happening."

"What is there to email? The struggle goes on and will continue to go on."

"Yes, I know." Now that sounded like the Paul she knew, Joan thought, always focused on the struggle.

"You know," Paul said, "once in Olancho you can never leave."

"I know, the people stay in your heart. And so will you," she hugged him and proceeded out the door.

Dave was anxiously watching for Joan to arrive as it got closer to eleven.

Don't worry, she'll be here, he told himself. Kathy was too busy saying goodbye to Santiago to notice his anxiety. They had both agreed that long distance relationships had no chance to survive, and both agreed they were going to try anyway. They just couldn't bring themselves to say it was over.

Dave was relieved to see Joan arrive a little after eleven. They had been waiting for her before going through customs.

"How'd it go?" he asked as he kissed her.

"I told him no," she said.

"Are you sure that's what you want to do?" Dave asked, relieved and yet afraid to be too relieved.

"Yes, I'm sure. There are poor people in America, too. God needs good people in America. I can serve God there as well as in Central America, maybe even more. Perhaps I can do more in my own country to better the lot of the Honduran people, of all people. And Honduras doesn't have you. I would miss you," Joan said, reaching up to touch his face.

"I would miss you too."

"It's means so much to me that you were willing to go along with this, if I had chosen to stay. Maybe that's all I needed to know," she said gazing into his eyes. "Besides, we can always come back."

"That we can," Dave agreed.

"Call me when you get home," Santiago said as they embraced one last time. "I'll be waiting for your call."

"I might get home before you," Kathy responded, thinking about the long drive he had ahead of him.

"I'll be thinking about you the whole time."

"Me too," Kathy said with a sigh, "Tell Anna and Sarah I said goodbye."

"Come on," Dave said, "we have to go."

They kissed as they said goodbye.

June 2006

"There they are," Kathy said as Joan, Dave and their sons disembarked from the plane at Juticalpa. She raced to greet them and hugged each.

"I couldn't get married without my favorite brother and his family," she said. She and Santiago had been right. Long-distance relationships just don't work. So after six frustrating months of phone calls and emails, Kathy had decided to put her home on the market and move to Catacamas. It would have been much harder for Santiago to move with his daughters, easier for her to move to Honduras. And she had always wanted the opportunity to use her Spanish more. Now she had it.

The wedding had been set for June, giving them ample time to prepare. Clemente was to preside at the wedding, with Paul assisting. It was a large church wedding, with all of Santiago's family, extended family, the whole town pretty much in attendance, followed by a large fiesta at the ranch.

Paul was as busy as ever, planning for the thirty first anniversary memorial. This time it would be simple, just a Memorial Mass.

"Never forget," he had said to her. "We must never forget the martyrs of the people."

Joan just smiled.

"Oh, and thank you for sending your sister," Paul said as Dave joined them.

"I think she sent herself. I didn't have anything to do with it," he responded.

"She is already making a difference. She's been helping out at the school and helping with Religious Education classes at the church. The children love her."

"Funny," Joan said, "here I thought I would be the one moving to Honduras. Who would have thought it would be Kathy," she said as she looked over at her, laughing, speaking Spanish with ease. "She looks happy."

"You will stay for the Memorial Mass," Paul said.

"Of course, wouldn't miss it," Dave said as he asked Joan for a dance. "You look happy, too," he told her.

"I am happy. So good to be here, good to see Kathy so happy."

"No regrets?" he asked.

"No regrets," she said.

"No nightmares?"

"Now and then, but that's okay. I want to remember."

"How could you forget? Remember, 'Olancho is easy to enter, hard to leave.' It remains in your heart."

"That it does."

*All quotes at the beginning of each section were taken from *Concientizacion, Evangelizacion, Politica*, by Leonidas E. Proaño, 1984, pp. 18-19, 37, 69 & 111.

Acknowledgements

Thank you to Fr. Richard Preston for sharing the story of his four years in Honduras with me. Without him this book would never have been written.

While based on true stories, the events in this novel have been fictionalized and are not to be read as historical fact. The murder of fourteen in Olancho is true; what actually happened that night in Horcones remains a mystery carried by those who died into their graves.

This book is dedicated to all of the missionaries in Central America and Latin America who have given up so much and put their lives in jeopardy in order to stand with the poor and speak God's word to God's people.

Thank you!

Q & A on *Land of Deep Waters*

Q – What led you to write this book?

A – Originally I had wanted to give people who had never lived in a third world country a chance to experience this. I also wanted to lead them through a process of consciousness-raising that can come from such experiences if one is open to the process. I spent the summer of 1980 in the Dominican Republic, living with two sisters there. This was my first experience with a third world country. I was deeply troubled by the experience and spent the year afterwards trying to come to some understanding of why there was such suffering in the world.

During this time I was friends with Fr. Richard Preston who had spent four years in Honduras. I interviewed him extensively about his years there and used his story as the basis for a book; however, what I had written back then was terrible. I kept it because I felt strongly about what I had wanted to do with the book. I believed in its importance. Thirty years later I picked the book up, discarded most of what I had written, kept what was worth keeping, and started again.

From the perspective of thirty years later, I found myself wondering how I had ended up where I was and questioning whether I had "sold out" because of my middle class life style. Hence I created Sr. Joan, someone who found herself looking at her middle class life style and wondering about the people she had left behind in Honduras. I decided to do the book as a retrospect and then added a fourth section, where Joan would return to Honduras.

Q – You start each section of the book with a quote. Why did you choose to do this?

A - Fr. Preston introduced me to the book, *Conscientization Evangelizacion, Politica,* by Leonidos Proaños. I found it spoke to what I had experienced after my summer in the Dominican

Republic. Proaños spoke of a three-part process of going to a third world country and allowing yourself to be touched deeply by the experience until it transformed you and led to action for change. That was the process I wanted to lead people through with this book.

Q – Why your title, *Land of Deep Waters*?

A – Honduras means land of deep waters. Even more important, the process of consciousness raising that I referred to takes one into a land of deep waters, the realm of the mind and the inner workings of the mind. As Proaños points out in his book, some people go to a third world country, see the suffering of the poor, then rush to provide relief through charity. While not a bad idea, they are acting more out of self-interest, to relieve their guilt, than out of an understanding and appreciation for the people. To allow the suffering of the people to sink deeply into our beings and be transformed by this is to enter a land of deep waters. Only after this does a person take effective action to alleviate suffering. Joan and Paul both entered these deep waters. They allowed the people of Honduras to change them, a change that lasted throughout their life.

Q – Besides your time in the Dominican Republic and interviews with Fr. Preston, how did you research this novel? Did you spend time in Honduras?

A – Unfortunately Honduras is not a safe place to visit at this time. Fortunately, through the Internet, there is a world of knowledge at our finger tips to supplement the information I received from Fr. Preston as well as my own experience in the Dominican Republic. I also traveled to Guatemala, neighbor to Honduras, to further give me a taste of life in Honduras. It is amazing to me that back in the 1980's when I had first gathered information on Honduras, the country of Guatemala, with its death squads, was one of the most dangerous countries in Central America, while Honduras was relatively safe. Now that has reversed with Guatemala being safe and Honduras being unsafe. All this is relative though as recent increases in gang violence in Honduras, Guatemala and El Salvador has resulted in a flood of children fleeing these countries. Such are the dynamics of Central America.

Q – Your book describes some horrific events; did these actually happen within the missionary experience in Central America?

A – Yes, these and more. The story of Central America includes a history of rape, torture, kidnapping and murder. Being associated with a church is no safeguard against the violence that is part of these countries. Bishop Oscar Romero of El Salvador was shot while in the middle of celebrating Mass. In 1980, three American nuns and a lay woman were raped and murdered in El Salvador. In sharing their lives with the people of these war torn countries, they also shared in the dangers. However the atrocities experienced by the people and the numbers of them killed, far exceed the numbers of missionaries killed.

Q – How has your own experience in third world countries affected you and does it continue to affect you?

A – As mentioned, I was deeply affected by my time in the Dominican Republic. Since that time I have tried to maintain a "preferential option for the poor" in my theology and life. This means I consider those who are most vulnerable in how I vote and in my own life decisions. I have consciously sought out those who are poor in my own country, working on a volunteer basis as chair for a non-profit, End Hunger in Jackson: The Jackson Food Pantry Association, for eight years, and in other volunteer capacities. I am living a middle-class lifestyle and yet rich in the eyes of many in third world countries. As such, I struggle with the same issues Joan struggles with in my book and continue to struggle with how to best live the gospel values I believe.

Note to the reader:

Did you enjoy reading this book? If so, please leave a review on Amazon. Your comments would be appreciated and mean so much to me in terms of helping others notice my book. You, the reader, have the power to make or break a book in this day of emarketing and social media.

Thank you so much for reading *Land of Deep Waters*. I hope that it gave you much to think about.

Patricia Robertson

www.ingramcontent.com/pod-product-compliance
Lightning Source LLC
Chambersburg PA
CBHW070953120726
47910CB00004B/1219